WAIT FOR THE WAKE

Noel didn't want Christina to die. Not really—although she was in love with her husband Jonas, she went away, putting as much distance between them as possible, and tried to forget him. But on seeing him again, Christina was afraid. She didn't know she had more reason to be afraid of someone else—someone who saw in Noel a perfect candidate for the act of murder.

MARGARET CARR

WAIT FOR THE WAKE

Complete and Unabridged

LINFORD
Leicester

First published in Great Britain in 1974

First Linford Edition
published August 1989

British Library CIP Data

Carr, Margaret, *1935–*
    Wait for the wake.—Large print ed.—
Linford mystery library
I. Title
823'.914[F]

    ISBN 0-7089-6736-1

Published by
F. A. Thorpe (Publishing) Ltd.
Anstey, Leicestershire
Set by Rowland Phototypesetting Ltd.
Bury St. Edmunds, Suffolk
Printed and bound in Great Britain by
T. J. Press (Padstow) Ltd., Padstow, Cornwall

*The characters in this book are
entirely imaginary and bear no
relation to any living person*

1

THE bus driver let her down with some misgivings. No one had ever asked to be dropped in the middle of nowhere before. He was new to the route and never in his life had he seen anywhere quite so desolate and lonely. Below the road, huge rolling sweeps of meadow and cultivated land went down into a valley where only an occasional farmhouse broke up the landscape. Above, a thick belt of trees went on up to the ridge, the tips showing black against the skyline. The girl dropped her suitcase over the drystone wall which hemmed the trees and laughed at the driver. "Don't look so worried. I was born in these parts. I know every stick and stone."

"But I am," the driver said. "And it's getting dark. Surely you're not going through the wood?"

"Yes. My home is over the ridge." She swung herself over the wall, a tall elegant girl with long legs and a striking face that no one would forget easily. She didn't look country

1

bred. She was a product of city life, smart, sophisticated and stylish. He couldn't see her tramping through mud, getting her clothes torn, her face scratched, her hair disarranged. "You'll be better going into the town," he said. "And getting a taxi. There must be a road out to where you live."

"This is quicker." She picked up her case. "Thanks for stopping," and in a moment she had disappeared through the trees.

He shrugged and got back into the bus. It was none of his business of course but he shouldn't have made an unscheduled stop. If anything happened to her and it came out . . . He shrugged again. Who could say no to a girl like that? That type always got what they wanted. And always fell on their feet. Nothing would happen to her.

She walked through the wood quietly and without haste, all her senses alive to the fact that she was on home territory again. She had played in this wood, she had created her own tree house, seen the first flowers of the spring —the pure discreet snowdrop, the pale yellow primrose, the mass of bluebells blanketing the ground in a deep blue haze, the crocus and the daffodil. Spring was always exciting. The rebirth, the renewal of hope, the promise of life. Now it was autumn. The leaves were thick beneath her feet, falling even as she walked, the last rays of the sun coating the rich reds and oranges with gold, their sharp tangy smell in her nostrils, subduing even the Fath perfume she wore.

She loved all the seasons. In New York they slipped by, unmarked, scarcely noticed, meaning nothing more than a change of clothes. She had been away for six years. It seemed like six centuries.

The farmhouse could be seen from the top of the ridge, nestling into the ground like a broody hen, the steep gabled rooftops protecting it from all weathers, the old grey stone walls bulging a little and giving it a curiously contented air, like a well-fed cat. Windyridge Farm had stood in its hollow for two centuries at least and for the last hundred and fifty years it had sheltered the Clare family through bad times and good. The Clare men were of sturdy yeomen stock with a love for their land and their families which rarely faltered. Their women were fitting mates—sensible, practical, able to put their hands to almost anything—and they brought their children up to respect the virtues they held high.

Only Noel Clare had not measured up to standard. She had been difficult as a child, stormy, precocious and passionately self-willed. Her school reports had been atrocious but whereas this wouldn't have mattered to most Clare girls, trained to be good wives, efficient in both the home and the farm, Noel soon showed what she thought of the idea of marrying one of the local boys. She wanted better than that.

And she'd got it too . . . and look what it had brought her! She cut through the long meadow, keeping close to the thick hawthorn hedge. Six years ago she'd left Windyridge vowing never to return. It had been over a year before she could bring herself to write and then her mother had never answered. She should have been apprehensive of her welcome, unsure of herself, but she was only glad to be home again. However they greeted her, blood was thicker than water. Hadn't it pulled her back when she had everything a girl could possibly want? And who was she trying to kid? It wasn't the blood ties that had pulled her back. She pushed that thought away and climbed over the stile and into the four-acre field. The sleek Jersey cows there regarded her curiously, ambling over for a closer look. The five-barred gate at the bottom had been mended. It opened easily without the struggle it used to take.

She crossed to the other side of the road automatically although in London she had constantly looked the wrong way when crossing the road. The habits formed when young were stronger than any others superimposed in later life.

Another five hundred yards and then the farmhouse itself. She stood for a moment at the gate. It had been freshly painted, as had the fence surrounding her mother's flower garden. She went into the yard. The cow shed had been extended and there was a new barn. Things must have improved. There'd been no money for that when she'd been at home. There was a soft neigh as she paused at the stables and she put down her case and lifting the heavy latch on the wooden door she went inside. A new hunter—a fine beast with wicked eyes, Rosemary's placid bay, even more placid than of yore, and her own darling Tempest, a light of welcome in his eyes. After six years he still knew her.

She pressed her cheek against him, rubbing her hand along his nose. "Tomorrow we'll fly, my darling. Have you missed me? Have they been looking after you?" She had raised Tempest herself, put him through his paces, won prize after prize with him at the local gymkhanas. There'd been a half fear that John might have sold him when she'd gone. He'd been capable of it. The strong disapproving male, with rigid principles and a narrow mind. He had been the one who had brought the whole thing to a head. He'd been the one to worry about what people might think and say. If he hadn't interfered . . . If. If. She shook her head at such thoughts. Maybe it had all been for the best. Sooner or later the realisation would have come. She'd been in love with Jonas Fenton and was probably the last person in Henton to know it.

She left Tempest and went round to the back of the farmhouse. The tables were still out on the paved patio where on fine days they would have their tea, looking out across the lawn to the brook at the bottom where the weeping willows played tag with the plump white ducks paddling in the clear waters.

The standard lamp was on behind the french

windows, its warm glow shining on the brasses her mother loved. The room seemed to be empty but the high winged chair her mother used had its back to her.

She opened the window and stepped inside. There was an abrupt movement from the chair but it wasn't her mother who jumped up to stare at her. It was a complete stranger, with silver blonde hair, bleached at that, though it was an expert job, as was the make-up, which emphasised brilliant green eyes and a wide full mouth.

Noel stared at her in astonishment. "Who are you?"

"I think that I should be asking that question." She had a cool languid voice. It suited her. She was wearing a long quilted housedress in a deep rose colour. There was a bottle of nail varnish in her hand, very nearly the same colour, and she had almost finished painting her finger nails. She put the bottle down and flipped open the lid of a cigarette box on the table beside the chair. "But I can make a guess. You must be Noel. You're very like Rosemary—or is it Rosemary is like you? I never know which is which. Cigarette?" She held the box out.

Noel shook her head. "No thank you."

"You're still wondering who I am?" She raised her brows, plucked and painted to perfection. "I'm Nicola Clare—your brother's wife."

"*You're* married to *John?*" It was rude but she couldn't help herself. The John she knew wouldn't have liked to be seen talking to a girl like this, to marry her was something so incredible that she just couldn't believe it.

Nicola didn't take offence. Instead she laughed. "I know . . . he's not changed—it was a momentary madness on his part. I don't think there's a minute of the day that he doesn't regret it now but divorce is out of the question of course in the Clare family. Sit down, won't you? Make yourself at home."

Noel sat down carefully. "Where is John?"

Nicola shrugged. "Out on the farm somewhere. He'll be in for dinner."

"And my mother?"

"In her room." Her eyes sharpened. They were fringed with lashes so thick and long they had to be false, but there was an expression in them that brought an acute apprehension to Noel. "I don't suppose you know," she said slowly. "Your mother had a stroke . . . oh, some years ago now. She's paralysed . . . almost

8

completely." She jumped up. "You look as if you could do with a drink." She opened a cupboard which had previously held a stack of knitting and dressmaking patterns but was now filled with bottles of spirits and wines. Noel's eyes widened. The only alcoholic beverage allowed in the house in her mother's time had been a half bottle of brandy for medicinal purposes.

"Scotch, I think," Nicola murmured, pouring a generous measure into a glass. "And soda?" She made a token squirt. "I'll get some ice."

Left holding the glass Noel looked around her. There were quite a few changes not at first apparent. The tapestry curtains had been changed to brocade, the wallpaper was more dashing than her mother would have chosen, the carpet was fitted and there were bright cushions scattered around. She got up and added more soda to her drink. There was a painting on the wall, a turbulent storm at sea with a ship heading for the rocks.

"Before you make any comment," Nicola said, coming up behind her with a vacuum jug filled with ice cubes, "I painted that and I'll slit the throat of anyone who says it's lousy."

"But it's very good."

"Surprise, surprise! You have a cute back-handed way of giving out compliments, don't you?" She dropped a couple of ice cubes in Noel's drink and sat down, stretching out her legs in front of her. There were fluffy mules on her feet and her toes showed. They'd been painted too. "If it's not a rude question," she said, "what have you come back for? A visit? Or were you thinking of coming back for good? Only this is my home now and I run it my way. You'll find things are different."

"And do I have to ask your permission to stay?"

Nicola's eyes narrowed. "Your sister used to speak to me in that tone of voice, looking down her nose at me as though I'd crawled out from under a stone. She soon changed her tune. I have a very pleasant nature, I'm easy to get on with and I can be very generous. *But* I don't like to be patronised or treated as if I'm of no account. If you stay here you'll find I'm a person to be reckoned with." She put down her glass with a sharp snap as if to emphasise her words and then smiled, "We'll start again now I've cleared the air. I see no reason why we shouldn't get on well together. You'd like your old room I suppose but I'm afraid you'll find it's changed. I had it done over as a guest room."

Noel felt a sharp pang. She didn't let it show but put down her untasted drink. "I'd like to see my mother now if you'll excuse me."

"Certainly. I'll show you up."

As if I were a stranger, Noel thought bleakly, following her down into the hall and up the broad shallow stairs that led to the first floor. Her mother's room had been at the front of the house but Nicola led her to the back. "We moved her next to Rosemary," she explained. "It's much more convenient for her and of course your mother has the better view here."

"Can she talk?"

"No, I'm afraid not. Rosemary spends a great deal of time with her. Wasting her life I tell her but she won't let me get a nurse in." She opened the door, switching on the light and walked slowly in saying brightly, "Look who I've brought to see you."

Esther Clare was propped up by a mound of pillows, her bed pushed up to the window. She had shrunk. She looked like a limp rag doll instead of her mother, even the narrow single bed seemed too big for her. Her eyes were

11

closed and Nicola clapped her hands. "Come on, Mother. Wake up."

"Let her sleep," Noel said quietly. "I'll wait here."

"It could be a long time." Nicola looked as if she were about to argue but changed her mind. "All right then. I've got to dress anyway. Dinner's at eight. John and I are going out but I'll tell Mrs. Cassell you're here and you can eat with Rosemary. She usually eats on a tray in here but she must make an effort in your honour tonight. I'll send her up as soon as she comes in. She borrowed my car and went shopping in Elmsbury this afternoon." She glanced at her wristwatch and frowned. "She should have been back before this."

Noel pushed her sleeve back and consulted her own watch. It was after six.

"That's a nice watch," Nicola said, stepping forward and examining it closely. "That must have cost a pretty penny."

"I suppose so," Noel said absently, her eyes on her mother. "Is Rosemary a good driver?"

"Rosemary?" Nicola laughed. "She's good at everything she does. Don't you know that? But of course she would still have been at school when you left home. Let me see . . . She's

twenty now so that made her thirteen or four-
teen then. I don't suppose you were all that
close—four years' difference at that age is a lot.
I expect Rosemary is more like a sister to me
than to you now. We're very close."

And yet she doesn't eat with you, Noel
thought. Aloud she said, "How long have you
been married?"

"Just over three years. I came down here for
the summer and met John and that was that.
We were married within the month. Well . . .
I'll leave you. Tomorrow we'll have a proper
talk. I'd like to know what you've been up to
all this time, and why people usually shut up
when your name is mentioned. What crime did
you commit that got you turfed out of here?"

"No crime," Noel said in level tones.

Nicola smiled. "Don't worry. I'll get it out
of you. I think you're going to be a far more
compatible companion than Rosemary. She is
really very conventional you know."

Rosemary. Long pigtails, a thin brown face,
a wiry body and hot hate-filled eyes. Rosemary
had taken John's side and it had hurt.

Noel sat down in the window seat at the
bottom of the bed and leaned her head on her
knees. Beyond the brook and across the fields

were the woods of Ridley Manor. The Fentons had lived there for far longer than the Clares had lived at Windyridge. They had lorded it over the people for miles around with powers of life and death in their hands. The portraits in the long gallery over the ballroom showed what kind of men those first Fentons had been. Strong, fierce, proud men. Too proud for their own good. They earned the enmity of the crown too many times to prosper and as the generations passed a weakness crept in the strain. The lands were sold to pay gambling debts, fresh infusions of money received with well dowried brides were soon squandered and by the turn of the century the Fentons were fighting for survival, having lost almost everything. But the one thing they could never lose was their appeal for women. Their wildness and dark good looks were a legend, every generation having a tale to tell the next, and when James Fenton looked like being the last of the line, heading for a pistol to the head and leaving a trail of gambling debts, there were many young women of fortune who would have been only too happy to oblige with their dowries. Unfortunately James had married young and if his wife couldn't produce any sons to continue the line she was otherwise disgustingly healthy. That is, until Adele Beaton appeared on the scene. She was from Boston, the daughter of a rich man who had seen to it that she got everything she wanted in her young life. And after one meeting with James Fenton she wanted him so much she couldn't rest until she'd got him. Adele saved the Fentons. She brought new blood into the family; her son Jonah had her ambition and her father's brains. He made money hand over fist and was able to recover a lot of the land they had lost. He married a lady, but his mother approved of the match which meant she was no meek, washed-out member of the English aristocracy but a girl of spirit with a personality that could stand up to Adele's.

She still lived at the manor. Lady Valerie, the mother of Jonas. Her husband, Jonah, had been killed in the first year of the war and Jonas had been born two months later. Things were difficult. There were the death duties and she listened to the wrong people and lost money, made bad investments, lost money again. By the time Jonas was twenty-one things were in a bad state again and there wasn't much left for him to inherit. He took the normal Fenton step of marrying a rich girl and went into business on her money. He had some setbacks but the American side of him didn't recognise them as such and by the time he was thirty he was a very rich man. His wife Christina resented this —as in fact she resented a great many things about her husband. She'd bought him. She expected him to stay to heel. But no Fenton had ever been a trained puppy dog and Jonas had the lean dark wildness of the first of the line. He had their pride too and after one stormy row which Christina precipitated he announced abruptly that he was leaving her. He did it there and then and realising too late that she would sooner have him as a part-time husband than not have him at all Christina went after him. Her car hit the parapet on the ridge road and she broke her back.

She'd been in a wheelchair when Noel had first met Jonas. She knew of him and she'd seen him occasionally but it had in no way prepared her for the impact of his personality. He'd gone back to Christina of course. One didn't desert a cripple. Life didn't hold much amusement for him, however, until he found that Noel could make him laugh again.

Had he known what he was doing? Noel looked out into the darkness. She didn't think so. It was something that had crept up on them. That first meeting out on the downs. She on Tempest and Jonas on his big fiery Hemlock. They had done nothing wrong, not then or all the other times they had met. It was enough to talk, to ride as if all the hounds of hell were chasing them, and then to relax and swim in the river or walk through the woods with the sun slanting down through the trees, producing dappled shadows which danced in front of them.

She had met him in the spring and before she could draw breath again it was winter and the snow was on the ground and John was telling her she was becoming the talk of the neighbourhood. He'd arranged for her to go up to Scotland to stay with an old uncle and aunt, renowned for their almost fanatical religious observance and the strict discipline which was imposed on anyone staying in their house. After a few months with them John considered she would listen to reason. Fred Garnett wanted to marry her. He was a good man, a friend of John's, and one day he'd have his own farm. Once Noel had some sense knocked into her she'd make a fine wife. All the Clare women made excellent farmers' wives. It was a well known fact and Noel wasn't going to spoil the record.

Only she hadn't gone to Edinburgh. She'd cashed her ticket in when she'd reached London and gone to the domestic agency she'd seen advertised in *The Lady*. She wanted to get as far away as possible. She wasn't going to Edinburgh, she wasn't going to marry Fred Garnett. She was in love with Jonas Fenton and as she couldn't marry him she wasn't going to marry anyone else.

It took time to arrange. She got a casual job to keep her going, washing dishes in a busy hotel. Only domestic work was open to her. She'd worked for the vet in Henton but answering the phone and soothing frightened, suffering animals wasn't much of a recommendation for a job in London. There didn't seem to be any vets there at all. She supposed they did exist. There were the horses in Hyde Park. She walked there the first Sunday morning but didn't go back. It was a poor substitute for a ride on Tempest across the open ground at full gallop but she still envied the riders. They were the kind of people Jonas would know, the people of his world. What had he done when he heard she'd been packed away? Anything? Did he care about her at all?

She sailed on Christmas Eve—her birthday. She'd been eighteen. And now she was twenty-four and she was home again.

She turned around and saw her mother's eyes were open. She lowered her feet to the floor and stood up slowly. "Hello, Mother."

Esther gave no sign that she knew her daughter. Her eyes were dull and lack-lustre.

Noel walked round the bed and sat on the edge of it, taking her mother's limp wasted hand in her own. "I guess I know why you didn't write back now. I'm sorry. If I'd known I'd have been back before this."

A solitary tear formed in her mother's eye and spilled out onto her cheek. It was followed by another and then another.

Noel plucked a tissue from the box on the bedside table and gently blotted her cheek. "Did you get my letter? Did you know I'd gone to America? Your training came in very useful. People thought I was a marvellous maid. They paid me well, provided me with my own room, sometimes my own bathroom. I've lived in luxury and done a lot of travelling and now I'm thinking of settling down. I've met a man, the son of some people I was working for. He's in television, a producer. I would have a very good life, so you see all your worries about me have come to nothing."

The tears continued to roll. Noel chattered on but she was beginning to get worried and looked up in relief when the door opened and Rosemary entered.

For the first moment Noel didn't recognise her. The plaits had gone, she had filled out and grown taller but the eyes were the same, hostile, hard, and filled with a bright anger as she demanded to know what Noel was doing.

"You've upset her. Look at her! She's never done that before." She pushed Noel aside so roughly she almost fell off the bed.

"I didn't say anything that could have upset her," Noel said defensively.

"You didn't have to, did you? The sight of you is enough. You always did mean trouble and I don't suppose you've changed. What have you come back for?"

"I'd have come back before if I'd known about Mother. When did it happen?"

"Not very long after you'd gone. What do you imagine your disappearance did to her? Did you think she didn't care? You always were her favourite and her pride and joy, yet you did nothing to deserve it. Nothing! While I—I did everything to make her love me."

Noel regarded her sister in silence and then turned on her heel and left the room. There was nothing she could say. Rosemary was eaten up with jealousy. She always had been.

She went to what had been her room and was glad Nicola had given her warning. It had been completely transformed. Nothing was out of place; drapes, cushion covers and counterpane matched, the bed was a new one, with a quilted headboard and sidetables, the carpet was a thick Axminster into which her feet sunk. It had cost a lot of money to make it what it was and it should have been a beautiful room of great charm but instead it was as coldly impersonal as a hotel room.

Someone had brought her case upstairs. She unlocked it and unpacked and then went along to the bathroom where she received another shock. That had received the transformation treatment too. The suite was coloured, the walls were mirrored and another fitted carpet covered the floor.

She had a bath, discovering as she sank down that the ceiling was mirrored too. Nicola certainly enjoyed the sight of her own body. She provided superb bath towels however. She had money, Noel decided. It was the only logical conclusion. John would never have been able to find it in his heart to lash out so lavishly. But then she didn't know Nicola. Maybe she had got the money out of him somehow. She certainly seemed determined to have her way in all things.

Noel changed into a long leisure gown and went downstairs to the kitchen. There was a girl with Mrs. Cassell; a youngster of about eighteen with a pert nose and wide knowing eyes.

Mrs. Cassell was bending over the stove, a sparse, greyhaired figure who had always looked the same ever since Noel could remember. Neat print cotton dresses even in the depth of winter, wrap-around aprons, hair in a bun, flat brogues and lisle stockings. She turned around and put her hands on her hips. "Well, well! You've done some growing up while you've been away. Aren't you the fashionable lady then! Madam Clare will have to look to her laurels."

Noel grinned. "It's good to see you, Mrs. Cassell. How have things been? Have you been keeping well?"

"I'm just fine and as to how things have been you'll see for yourself. I've got help—that's an improvement. This here's Sharon."

"Hello, Sharon."

The girl smiled. She was making butter balls, rolling them dexterously between the wooden paddles.

"Madam Clare doesn't believe in doing any housework herself," Mrs. Cassell said with some malice. "Oh, she'll do the flowers. No one else can make it a work of art. Did you know she was an artist?"

"I saw the painting on the wall."

"Yes. She thinks she's good. Spends most of her time at it." She sat down at the long kitchen table with its scrubbed top. "Make a cup of tea for us, Sharon, there's a good girl, and sit down, Noel. I don't suppose you've had a real welcome from anyone. You've seen your mother?"

"Yes."

"A sad thing. It would have been better if she'd gone there and then. There's been no improvement in all this time. She's a vegetable —and poor Rosemary—devoted to her she is. Never leaves her for long at a time. She feeds her and washes her and does everything for her.

23

Won't let anyone else touch her." Without a change of expression, not even a pause for breath, she went on, "Would you like a slice of my angel cake, Noel? You always were partial to it. But no, you'll be eating in another half hour, best not to spoil your appetite." She picked up the teapot and poured. "You've not seen your brother then?"

"No."

"He's right there." Mrs. Cassell made a graphic gesture with her thumb. "He never knew what hit him."

"Who is she? Where did she come from?"

"She was staying with the Nevilles. You won't know them, they're new to the district. *He's* a writer and *she* opened a pottery shop in the village—all hand-made stuff. A peculiar woman, but smart—very smart. He's got the money there but I doubt if he gets it from his books. No one's ever heard of him. He's an attractive man and, as a matter of fact, we all thought at first that Madam Clare had her eye on him. She was a widow, married a man in his sixties and didn't take long to see him off. We don't know what she did before that."

"Dear me—your espionage system falling

down?" Noel sipped her tea. "Do you call her madam to her face?"

"Certainly. She insists on it."

"Where's she gone tonight?"

Mrs. Cassell didn't answer right away. She got up and bustled over to the stove, giving a stir to one of the bubbling pans, then she said casually, "Go down to the cellar, Sharon, and get a bottle of Barsac. You'd like some wine with your meal, wouldn't you, Noel?"

Noel's brows went up and Mrs. Cassell nodded. "Yes, indeed! We live like the nobs now, people to dinner, cocktail parties, all that sort of thing—we had to have a wine cellar." She paused for a moment as Sharon opened the cellar door and went down the stone steps and then lowering her voice said, "They're up at the manor. There's a big shindig there tonight. Lady Valerie is sixty today. Not that Madam Clare is on more than nodding terms with *her* but she's got very friendly with Christina. And we all have our own ideas about that." She eyed Noel significantly.

Noel kept her voice dead level. She wasn't going to be trapped into any unwary statement whether Sharon was there or not. Mrs. Cassell knew her too well. "And what's that?" she said.

Mrs. Cassell wasn't going to spell it out. "He's away a lot of course," she said. "Paris, Brussels, Berlin, the Scandinavian countries. All this Common Market business. But he was in America this summer. For almost two months."

Noel's heart jumped violently but she'd had nearly seven years' training in concealing her emotions. She said mildly, "Are you talking about Jonas Fenton?"

Mrs. Cassell didn't go to the trouble of confirming the obvious. "I saw the labels on your case but don't worry, I won't breathe a word."

"Breathe a word of what?"

"She doesn't know. We might talk, but not to strangers."

"Mrs. Cassell, I don't have the faintest idea of what you're talking about." She finished her tea quickly. She was getting out fast before Mrs. Cassell's imagination really went flying sky high.

"Does he know you're back?"

"Who?"

"Don't fence with me, Noel," Mrs. Cassell said gently. "I've known you since you were in rompers and you can't hide anything from me.

He's the reason you've come back. You can't forget him, can you?"

"It's not true. I'm going to be married at Christmas. I came home to see my mother."

"And you're not going to see him?"

Noel stared at her and then without a word turned and left the kitchen. Of course she was going to see him. She couldn't wait to see him. How could she marry Doug when Jonas still haunted her dreams?

2

THE big, heavy cumbersome furniture in the dining room had been replaced by a more elegant suite in rosewood. The table was round and two places were laid upon it; napkins, gleaming silver, slender wine glasses, mats of painted country scenes. It looked very much a scene out of Ideal Home.

As Noel stood eyeing it Rosemary came down. She had changed into a light woollen dress and put some makeup on, combing her hair into a heavy pageboy style which framed her face and then fell to her shoulders.

It gave Noel an odd sensation to look at her. They were alike—and yet so different. The same colouring, dark brown hair, brown eyes, a slightly olive cast to the skin. Rosemary was a little taller, thicker in the thigh and ankle with the trim muscular body of a PT instructor. She looked sturdy and capable, a true Clare, without any claim to beauty but an attractive girl for all that. Yet when she looked at Noel the already strong flames of resentment couldn't fail to be fanned into something stronger. The little differences between them, in themselves nothing, added up to an elusive quality that made Noel stand out. The slanting eyes, the rich full mouth, the way she moved, the supple grace of her body that didn't look strong enough to weather a strong wind, yet could hold a stallion like Tempest under control.

"Why have you come back?" Rosemary said coldly.

"You've already asked me that. Why didn't you let me know about Mother?"

"Why should I? I didn't think you cared. Besides John destroyed your letter. You won't get the prodigal's welcome here. I wouldn't be surprised if he turfed you out right away."

Noel shrugged and sat down. "In that case I'd better eat a hearty meal. When will he be back?"

"One . . . two o'clock. It depends on how much Nicola is enjoying herself. She'll be a little out of her element tonight."

Sharon came in with a steaming tureen of soup. She ladled it out and retreated without saying a word.

Rosemary slipped into the other seat and

picked up her spoon. "No questions? Can you imagine Nicola out of her element anywhere?"

"At the manor, yes."

"Oh—she told you where she was going?"

"No. Odd, wasn't it? I would have thought her the type to boast about it."

"Don't make the mistake of summing up Nicola in five minutes. She's a little more complex than that."

Noel broke her roll in two. "How do you get on with her?"

"We understand one another." Rosemary pushed her plate to one side. "You've been talking to Mrs. Cassell, haven't you? What has she told you?"

"Nothing very much."

"Don't give me that. I bet you caught up on the whole history of the place in ten minutes. You always were a favourite of hers. What did she tell you about me?"

"She said poor Rosemary has no life of her own. She won't let anyone else do a thing for Mother—and if you're interested—Nicola said something very similar but also added you wouldn't hear of her getting a nurse in. Do you fancy yourself in the role of martyr or is it a way out of working for a living?"

"What a vile thing to say," Rosemary said, half rising to her feet and then subsiding again.

"I suppose it was," Noel agreed calmly. "So you do it all for love! Mother wouldn't thank you for it. Why aren't you at the party tonight?"

"You must be joking! It's hardly entertaining watching Nicola make a fool of herself over your precious Jonas. I suppose you saw him this summer. Is that why you've come back here?"

Noel put down her soup spoon. Was it written all over her in letters a foot high or something? "He is not my precious Jonas," she said, fighting for calmness. "And America is a big country. The entire population of Henton could pay a visit and I'd be none the wiser."

Rosemary opened her mouth to make a retort but at that moment Sharon came in again loaded up with dishes. She removed the soup plates and put oval platters before them with a grilled steak covering fully half the space. The vegetable dishes held creamed and chipped potatoes, peas and cauliflower cheese.

Rosemary helped herself first, grimly pushing over the dishes to Noel. "Six years ago you'd have blasted me for saying that," she remarked. "But you're no more convincing now than you

31

were then. He came here you know, when you'd gone. He and John nearly came to blows and I think he leads Nicola on simply for the pleasure of raising John's blood pressure."

"Perhaps you'd like to see a picture of the man I'm going to marry." Noel opened her bag and pushed a photograph of Doug across the table. She wasn't surprised when Rosemary's eyes widened. Doug was a handsome man and the picture had been taken in Florida where every colour was emphasised; his tan was a deep mahogany, his eyes a dazzling blue while the sun had turned his blond hair to an almost silver hue which photographed superbly.

He'd been out fishing and was gutting a tarpon when she'd caught him. The silver was reflected in the scales of the fish and the gleam of the knife blade. As photographs went she reckoned it quite a poetic composition. The boat and the sea and sky, the man, tough and lean and worthy of a place beside any Steve McQueen or George Peppard pin-up. Even Doug had been impressed with it. He'd had half a dozen enlargements made.

She saw the uncertainty on Rosemary's face as she pushed it back across the table. Jonas wasn't handsome. His face was hard and craggy, a portrait of severe lines. He was taller than Doug and broader on the shoulders but as far as looks went Doug left him standing.

"Who is he?" Rosemary said flatly.

"His name is Doug Brominsky. He was an actor but now he's on the production side in television. There's more money in it and more prestige."

"How did you meet him?"

"I was working for his parents. They had a house on Long Island and he visited quite often, then last summer we went to Florida. He came down for a weekend and stayed for nearly a month. That picture was taken there."

"Didn't his parents object to your . . . friendship?"

Noel ignored the intended slur. "Funnily enough they were very pleased about it. English girls have a good name out there—steady, reliable, non-emancipated. They're of Polish stock. They don't like this equality of the sexes. A woman should know her place."

"And you know yours? That's a change!" Rosemary uttered a short laugh but she picked up the photograph again and took another look at it. "Will he be coming here?"

"No."

"Oh? Ashamed of us?"

"How can you say that?" Noel said gently. "Such a loving, devoted family, packing me off into the wilds of beyond to a bigoted old couple who would probably have fed me on bread and water and locked me in my room at night. And why? Because some old gossips had nothing better to do than invent a story that didn't hold even a grain of truth." She got up from the table. The steak was excellent but she couldn't have eaten another morsel. "I'm going to bed. I've been travelling a long time to get here—to get home. Home!" She smiled without humour and left the room.

Her mother was asleep. She looked in on her way back from the bathroom. She shouldn't have come home. It had been a mistake.

The bed was comfortable. She fell asleep almost immediately but was awakened by the sound of angry voices. Nicola and John. In the next room from the sound of things.

She put the pillow over her head. It was no concern of hers if they wanted to wake the household but then a violent expletive from John made her sit up sharply. He could turn her out but not at this time of the night. She got up and went to the bedroom door. There was no bolt on it. She hesitated, wondering whether to drag the chest of drawers across, but Nicola's voice, strident and a little slurred, stopped her dead.

"Why shouldn't I have told him? It was bound to come up in the course of any conversation. I must have told a dozen people or more."

John's voice, low and hard. She couldn't quite catch what he said but Nicola laughed. "So I didn't tell you. From the way you act every time I mention her name anyone would think she had the plague. I wanted to find out what she'd done for you to disown her."

Noel opened the door to hear better.

John said, "And did you?"

"I heard she was wild and uncontrollable. That her mother had never been able to do anything with her, that you were the one who sent her away and she ran off and no one has ever heard a word of her since. Everyone was very curious to know where she'd been and what she'd been doing. I learned more tonight from their questions than anything I managed to glean during the years I've been married to you."

"I'm not having her in this house. She can go right back to wherever she came from."

"So you keep saying, my dear John, but that's not good enough. Even Lady Valerie asked about her. If we threw a party for her I don't think the excuses will be so much in evidence. They'll come to see her and then I'm in. I'm sick and tired of being only on the fringe of things here."

"And who do you think you'll lure in this house? Jonas Fenton for one?"

"Why do you dislike him so much? Don't you realise that he's the most important man in the district and he makes you look a fool? It's not surprising people laugh at you. And don't try and tell me that it's because of me. You don't care when any other man pays me some attention."

"Oh don't I? You'll drive me mad one day, Nicola. I'm warning you. You think you can wind me round your little finger but there's a limit for any man. There's going to be no party and Noel is not staying here."

Nicola's voice dropped. Noel had to strain her ears. "You want that new tractor, don't you, John? And if I buy that for you, surely you can't begrudge my having a little party.

Don't you want to be accepted here? Don't you want to be proud of me? Noel won't be staying long. She's not the type. She's a city girl now. There'll be nothing for her here. Are you worried about her finding out about that money? That's it, isn't it?"

"What are you talking about?" John said, flurried and scared.

"I'm not stupid, John. I read the will. What are you going to do when Rosemary is twenty-one? Are you hoping for a miracle or do you think she won't find out either?"

"Rosemary will get what is due to her. It's different with Noel. She doesn't deserve it. She left the farm. She lost any rights she had here." The words tumbled out thick and furious. He believed them, that was what made it worse. They weren't excuses thought up on the spur of the moment.

Noel closed the door and got into bed. She wouldn't be turned out. Nicola would see to that. But once she'd served her purpose Nicola would act with the same ruthless efficiency in speeding her departure.

She glanced at her little travel clock. It was almost three. She picked it up and set the alarm for six and then lay on her back. Sleep didn't return easily. John had not only deprived her of a home but he had cheated her in some way and he had filled his mind with hate for her to justify it. She should have felt anger or perhaps contempt but instead she felt sorry for him.

He'd been sixteen when their father died and immediately all the problems and anxieties of running the farm had fallen on his shoulders. It must have been hard for him. He'd had no fun, none of the usual pastimes of youth. And he'd had the responsibility of his two sisters as well. She'd been ten then and was already proving too much for her mother. No, she couldn't find it in her heart to blame him. Now she was older she could understand.

The alarm went off in her ear and she shot up and cut it short in a flurry of bedclothes. Sleep had overtaken her unawares. The house was quiet. She listened but it didn't seem as if the noise had disturbed anyone. Sliding out of bed she trod softly to the window and pulled the curtains back. It was still dark. She had a quick wash and put on trousers and a black sweater. They'd probably burned her riding clothes along with all her other belongings. The complete disownment.

She pulled back the bolts on the front door.

If she used the back Mrs. Cassell would probably have a blue fit and start a cry of burglars.

The darkness was beginning to thin but the air cut like a knife. She crossed into the yard and opened the stable door. She could saddle Tempest blindfold which was just as well. She didn't dare put the light on and risk discovery. No one was going to stop her. Not today. Not this first morning when he knew she was back.

She led Tempest out and slid onto his back. He remembered the way. The sober sedate walk through the woods to the crest of the ridge. By the time they were on the top the sun was streaking the sky with pink and she leaned forward and whispered in his ear the words of long ago.

There was no other sensation in the world quite so good. The feeling that she and Tempest were one, cutting through the wind and air, the earth flying past them, the hedges no obstacle but a challenge, Tempest soaring over them as if he truly had wings.

She stopped him at the river and looked back. Silhouetted against the now rosy sky was another figure on horseback, bent low in the saddle and riding flat out as she had been.

He had come then. Somehow she had known

he would. She lost sight of him as he turned off the ridge. She was trembling, not with the cold now, but with an inner excitement that made her throat dry. He took the last hedge, soaring over it like a bird, checking his horse and approaching her at a slow canter.

It was odd. Noel felt as if she had been waiting all her life for this moment and all at once she couldn't bear it.

She turned and urged Tempest across the river and up the bank, over into the meadow and up the hill.

She could hear the thud of hooves on the ground behind her as Jonas slowly but surely decreased the distance between them. She threw a quick glance over her shoulder. He was smiling, his teeth very white against his swarthy skin.

"Come on, Tempest. To the tower."

Jonas caught up just before the drawbridge and his big bay edged Tempest onto it, his hand coming over to grasp the reins and pull them to a halt.

He dismounted without haste and reaching up put his hands around Noel's waist.

She looked down at him, tracing the differences the seven years had made in him; the silvery streaks in his black hair, the deepened furrows around his mouth, the hard line of his lips, even his eyes . . . they were dark and intent and had the look of a man who was dreaming.

She brought her leg over and with a long sigh slid down into his waiting arms.

It was no use. She could never marry Doug. This man held her heart and even the long absence away from him had brought no release.

"I can't believe it," he said slowly. He brought his hand up, tracing the curve of her cheek. His voice was deep and husky. "Noel . . ."

She didn't say anything. She reached up and brought his head down, standing on tiptoe to meet his lips with the kiss she had given him many times in her dreams. It was not the same. This time she could feel his arms around her, bruising her ribs, holding her so tightly she could hardly breathe. She could feel the beat of his heart, the rasp of his breath on her cheek, the hard, fierce demand of his mouth.

I love you, I love you. I love you. The sky was turning somersaults, the earth was vibrating beneath her, she was lost and she was reborn.

"Why didn't you write to me?" The awakening was just as big a shock as the alarm clock in the morning.

There was no tender light of love in his eyes, only a dark anger.

"I did—hundreds of times—but they all ended up the same way. What could I say? 'I love you, I want to marry you, come and take me away from here?'" She met his eyes steadily. "You treated me like a child, I could have been your kid sister. Nothing you ever said or did gave me any claim on you—not even to write and tell you where I was. Besides . . . there was Christina."

"Yes . . . Christina." He dropped his hands. "And you're getting married at Christmas."

"Who told you that?" she asked sharply.

"Rosemary. She showed me his picture. He looks a fine man. I hope you'll be happy."

His photo. Of course! She stared at Jonas. She'd left it on the table. Rosemary must have gone straight out to the party to show it to Jonas. But why? Why? Had she thought it would keep Jonas away from her?

"I'm not going to marry him," she said slowly. "Not now. I had to know for sure, you see. That's why I came back. To find out if I'd built something out of nothing. It's so easy to dream. I was young. It could have been the fantasy of a child, the way they pick on some pop idol and swear undying love, then a couple of years later wonder what on earth they saw in him. I loved you, Jonas, but I never knew it. Not until they told me they were sending me away because of you. It was like having my heart torn out. I thought I'd die. Never to see you again, never to laugh with you, never to—" Her voice broke. She took a deep breath. "But I thought I'd get over it. A new life, new people. It seemed the right thing to do. Only I couldn't forget you. Silly of me, wasn't it? I don't suppose you gave me more than a passing thought now and then."

"A little more than that." He smiled wryly. "Only it was a long time before I'd admit to myself that I loved you. You *were* a child. I'd not thought of you in any other way. And now—"

"I'm not a child any longer," she cut in swiftly.

"No . . . I can see that. What are we going to do, Noel?"

"Do we have a choice?"

"There's always a choice."

"No, I don't think so. I shall stay here a few days and then I'll go back. If you're ever free you'll know where to find me."

"I have to be free?"

"Yes, Jonas. I won't share you like Christina did."

She put her foot in the stirrup and swung herself on Tempest's back. He put his hand on the bridle. "I'll talk to Christina today. Let me take you to dinner tonight."

"What? And start all the gossip again? I had to mention Doug because everyone seems to take it for granted I came back because of you."

"Do you care what other people think?" He smiled a little and she returned it after a moment. Of course she didn't. Had she ever?

"I'll be waiting for you at eight o'clock."

"So be it." He slapped Tempest on the rump and she rode off alone. Slowly now. She had a lot to think about.

The yard was a hive of activity when she got back. The big hunter was being saddled and John was striding about shouting orders to three of the men. Rosemary was there and Nicola too, both standing frozen as if some tragedy had taken place. As she rode in Nicola screamed and ran forward. "Get off my horse. How dare you! Riding off without a word to anyone."

"*Your* horse?" Noel dismounted stiffly. It had been a long time since she had ridden. She glanced at John. "Have you disposed of *everything* that was mine?"

His dark face coloured. He was a big man with the shoulders of a bull and his head seemed too small for the rest of his body. He had the Clare dark colouring but his eyes were set close together and his mouth was a prim, tight purse. "We didn't know what had happened. You had no right to take him."

"And you couldn't guess? What were you going to do? Scour the countryside for me? Where's the horse whip? You weren't going to forget that, were you?"

She led Tempest into the stables and started to unsaddle him.

"Don't do that," Nicola said sharply. "One of the men can do it and make sure he's all right."

"Oh, he doesn't damage easily, Nicola. I didn't send him headlong at any six foot stone walls and he knows me. If you think I'm going to apologise you can take a running jump yourself. Tempest is mine and while I'm here I'm going to ride him."

45

"John, tell her. That horse is mine now."

"I warned you," he said sourly. "It's on your own head." He turned away.

Nicola bit her lip. "I don't mind your borrowing him," she said. "If only you'd asked first."

"You came in a little late last night. I didn't think you'd relish an early awakening."

"Oh! You heard us?"

"It was very illuminating."

Nicola put her hand to her mouth.

"Yes." Noel smiled. "I'll be here about a week. If you want that party you'd better start getting organised." She walked up to Rosemary. "I'd like my photograph back if you don't mind. It wasn't intended for public display."

"It's in your room."

"How very thoughtful of you. Considerate too. I hadn't suspected you possessed such qualities. It all goes to show, doesn't it?"

"What do you mean?"

"Oh, you know, Rosemary. You know very well."

She went in the kitchen by the back door and sat down at the table with a sigh. "Any breakfast going, Mrs. Cassell?"

"Started already, have you?" Mrs. Cassell stood with her arms crossed, shaking her head. "Trouble is your name. It always was and it looks as if it always will be. Did you see him then?"

"Who?"

"You didn't have that light in your eyes last night. If I were you I'd go and have a cold shower and be pretty smart about it before Madam Clare starts putting two and two together."

Noel laughed. "I want a double helping of everything. Bacon, eggs, mushrooms, tomatoes and sausages. I've just realised! I've not had a proper meal for three days."

"And what was wrong with that steak last night then?"

"Rosemary! She took my appetite away." Noel got up. "I'll have that shower but don't bank on it dousing any flames." She paused at the door, smiling impishly at Mrs. Cassell. "If you really expect fireworks hang around at eight o'clock. I'm being called for."

"Is he really coming here?" Mrs. Cassell demanded when she got down again, her face shining and her hair brushed back into a pony tail again. She'd lost the clasp around it. When?

When Jonas had kissed her? Every time she thought about it her stomach turned over.

"Yes."

"Isn't that rather foolish?"

"Foolish and fantastic and fabulous and—and, oh, I don't know."

She sat down again. If she could talk to anyone it had to be Mrs. Cassell. And if she didn't talk she'd blow up. It was boiling inside her like a volcano.

"What about this man you said you were marrying?" Mrs. Cassell said dourly.

"I've changed my mind."

"Child! Child! Do you know what you're doing?" Mrs. Cassell was shaking her head again as she emptied the frying pan and put a loaded plate in front of Noel. "He's a married man."

"He can very easily get unmarried." Noel laughed. She didn't want to listen to any wet blanketing. "Christina will give him a divorce."

"You've never met her, have you?"

"What's that got to do with it?"

"She's a determined woman."

"Well, the divorce laws are different now. It's easier."

"Not when you're up against someone like

48

Christina. She's got a big hold on him. If she was able to walk now it would be different but a cripple in a wheelchair . . ." Mrs. Cassell pursed her lips. "It takes a mighty strong man to turn his back on that."

"I don't want to know." She dug into the bacon and eggs but her appetite had gone again. She was glad when Nicola walked in. It gave her an excuse to push her plate aside.

"Making yourself at home, are you?" Nicola said tartly. "What's wrong with eating with us in the proper place?"

"I thought you'd have eaten."

"Well, I haven't—not yet. I wouldn't even have been up if it hadn't been for you. Are you in the habit of taking rides at dawn?"

"It's the best time. No one about, the countryside fresh, the dew still on the ground. Have you not found that out?"

"No," Nicola said shortly. "I'd like some coffee, Mrs. Cassell—black. You'll join me, Noel?"

It was an order not a request but Noel smiled sweetly. "Of course."

"Where's Sharon?" Nicola turned back to Mrs. Cassell.

"She was doing the sitting room."

49

"Good. We'll go there then. She'll have lit the fire."

It wasn't much of one. Nicola poked at it muttering, "Can't get a decent girl in this back of beyond for love nor money. And the wages I have to pay her!"

"Allow me." Noel bent down and in a few minutes had it drawing well. "I'm surprised you've not had central heating put in," she murmured. "You've made so many other improvements."

Nicola eyed her suspiciously, obviously suspecting sarcasm. "I like an open fire."

"Don't we all?" Noel dusted her hands. "I'll just nip upstairs for my cigarettes."

She came down again just in time to hear Sharon saying, "It's for Miss Noel, madam. Mrs. Cassell said she didn't like it black."

"Oh! All right then, leave it."

"Thank you, Sharon." Noel smiled at her and picked up the coffee pot. "Sugar, Nicola?"

"No."

"Counting the calories?" Noel added cream and sugar to her cup and sat down, aware how much she was adding to Nicola's resentment.

"You do know that if I hadn't intervened

John would have thrown you out this morning?"

"Oh? From the sound of it I thought it was going to be last night. How much money is involved? I suppose you know down to the last penny."

"So you heard that too."

"Didn't you remember I was next door? The walls are thick but you *were* shouting rather."

"I wouldn't put it past you to have been listening outside the door."

"The temptation to listen when you hear your own name is overwhelming. Cigarette?"

"I have my own." Nicola got one from the box, jumping a little as Noel snapped her lighter in her face. "What are you going to do about it?" she demanded.

"Nothing at all unless John drives me to it. I, too, am very easy to get on with." She smiled and after a moment Nicola said thoughtfully. "Don't you need the money?"

"No."

"It's quite an amount—ten thousand pounds."

"As you say—quite an amount—especially if you have to find it in a hurry. But you'd go to his rescue, wouldn't you, Nicola? After all, he is your husband."

The complete blankness on Nicola's face was almost laughable. Noel added smoothly, "But of course you'll make sure that he doesn't do anything that would send me off to a solicitor's and then the situation will never arise."

"I can't control your brother completely."

"Indeed? I thought you did very well last night."

Nicola inhaled deeply and surprisingly she laughed. "He doesn't always need a new tractor."

"Inconvenient," Noel said gravely.

"Yes." She leaned forward and stubbed out her cigarette. "About that party—have you any objections?"

"None at all. If it will make you happy, go right ahead."

"How about Saturday? That will give us three days to get ready for it."

"Fine by me."

"And I thought we'd have a dinner party tomorrow. Just a few people. Christina Fenton and her husband, Lady Valerie and Dr. Shepherd. And the Nevilles. You won't know them—they're friends of mine and new to the district."

"I believe Christina is a friend of yours too?"

"Yes. She's a marvellous person but I expect you know that. She doesn't allow anyone to pity her and she's wonderfully mobile in that wheelchair of hers. She can drive too. I admire her tremendously."

"Has she been here?"

"Of course—many times."

"And her husband?"

"Oh, Jonas is a busy man. He's away a great deal and he and John had some silly disagreement some time or other. I've never asked him here before but I think I can persuade John to see reason now."

"I *would* make sure before you extend any invitations."

Nicola laughed again. "While you're here I think I could get away with murder. Would you mind not mentioning that you know about the money? I'll make it up to you. I'll tell you what. I'll give you half—cash, no trouble. I doubt it you'd get that much if you went to court. John really is flat broke—or at least he has no ready money."

"I don't want your money."

"No one turns down money," Nicola said with conviction. "Maybe you think I don't mean it. I've plenty. My husband—my first husband that is—left me set up for life."

"How very nice for you."

Nicola groaned and cast her eyes upwards. "Don't speak to me in that tone of voice again, *please*. I said something vulgar, did I? I'm sorry, I can't help it. There's nothing devious about me. Forgive me? Just when the atmosphere was warming up too."

Noel couldn't help it. She had to laugh.

"That's better," Nicola said in approval. "Look, I'm sorry about this morning. It was a bit of a shock to be told Tempest was gone and we didn't think of looking in your bedroom until Rosemary suggested it and the way she did it put my back up straight away. Poor girl though. She was probably still suffering from last night. Jonas is very good with her but I've told him over and over again that kindness isn't the treatment for a lovestruck girl. I thought she was learning some sense when she refused to go to the party but I might have known she'd be unable to resist the temptation of seeing him. He tells me she turns up in the oddest places."

"And what happened last night to upset

her?" Noel got up to pour some more coffee, keeping her face averted.

"Well, I don't know exactly. She made a bee line for him as soon as she arrived—but that was normal enough. Only Jonas suddenly looked as if he was going to throttle her. He actually grabbed her, and then he walked away leaving her stranded with everyone staring at her. She rushed out with the whitest face I've ever seen. Everyone was talking about it but even I didn't dare ask Jonas what it was all about. He looked as if he would have cut the throat of anyone who dared to talk to him. He's a strange man, rude and overpowering at times, but there's something about him. But of course you know him, don't you?"

Noel had the sudden conviction that Nicola was playing with her. That she knew the way she felt and had told her about Rosemary deliberately, the implication that she knew Jonas better than most delicately planted for a reason. But that was silly. She wasn't devious, she'd said so herself.

She turned around and said evenly, "Yes, I know him." But that wasn't true. She didn't know him at all. She had made up a dream man. Of the real man she knew very little and the facts that were public knowledge should have been enough warning for her to leave right away and never see him again. Only she couldn't. She was just like Rosemary. Rosemary and how many others?

3

SHE left Nicola busily compiling a list of names for the party and went up to see her mother. Rosemary was feeding her something that looked like bread and milk. "Go away," she said.

"Stop acting like a child," Noel said wearily. "I'll stay with her and you can have a free morning."

"To do what?"

"How should I know what you like doing? Go and buy a new dress. Nicola is throwing a party on Saturday."

"I don't need a new dress."

"Wonderful for the morale." Noel brought a chair over and sat down.

"I hate you," Rosemary said in a low voice vibrant with feeling. "What did you have to come back and spoil things for?"

"What have I spoiled?" Noel asked warily.

"You know. You've seen him already, haven't you? You met him this morning. And I believed you yesterday. It was all a load of moonshine, wasn't it? *Wasn't it?*" She was almost crying. "He looked at me as if he could have murdered me. I knew then that it had all been a lie. You're going to take him away. I'll never see him again."

"You're not losing anything," Noel said in a low voice.

"And how do you know? What makes you so sure he's been living like a monk while you've been away? He liked me—I know he did." She dashed her hands across her eyes. "All right then. You finish this. I'll be back after lunch." She thrust the bread and milk into Noel's hands and almost ran from the room.

Noel closed her eyes. She felt sick. She took a deep breath and resumed the spooning of the pobs into her mother's mouth. It trickled out between her lips and she had to use the napkin constantly. Her mother had been so fastidious. What was she thinking now? How could she bear it? Could she think? And take in what was said? The lack-lustre eyes were fixed on her the whole time. Was it her imagination or was there some expression in them?

She put the empty bowl down. It had to be her imagination. She sought for words, some cheerful talk, and could find nothing to say.

She and her mother had never been particularly close. They had never talked—not the way of real conversation—and when her mother had sided with John in sending her away it had seemed a terrible betrayal. "I'm just going for my writing pad," she said. "I won't be a moment."

Her writing materials were in her case. She hadn't locked it again. She hadn't expected anyone to go through it. But someone had. She was a meticulous and careful packer. She'd performed the task for too many people to be anything else. Her writing case had been in the corner, and it had been there when she'd got the packet of cigarettes out of the carton that morning. Nicola or Rosemary? No, that was silly. Why should they? It was probably Sharon being curious when she cleaned her room. The bed had been made. She must have been in.

She opened the pouch where she kept her jewellery. She had some good pieces; gifts from her employers, and Doug was generous. He liked buying her presents. Nothing was missing. She checked her handbag. Wallet, traveller's cheques, diary, a couple of Doug's letters. She paused. The envelope was missing from one of them. Had she thrown it away? She couldn't remember.

She went thoughtfully back to her mother's room.

There might be no expression in her eyes but she'd been waiting for her. They followed her around the room.

"What is it, Mother? Do you want something?" She sat on the edge of the bed. Her mother's gaze had fallen to her writing pad. "You want to write something?" She took the top off her fountain pen and placed the pad in front of her mother, putting the pen between her fingers. They remained lax and helpless, unable to grip.

Noel curled her fingers round her mother's and put the pen to paper but there was still no reaction. She glanced up and saw her mother had fixed her gaze to her left hand. "You want to try the other?" She went through the same procedure with the left hand and this time she could feel the slow agonised movement of forefinger and thumb as they strained for a grip around the pen. She put the paper up, hardly breathing as it traced a wavering course across it. But it was illegible, a mere senseless scribble.

"Try again," she said cheerfully. "It's bound

to be difficult at first. It's hard enough for anyone normally righthanded to switch to the left."

Her mother tried three more times before the pen fell from her fingers and she proved incapable of holding it any longer. "We'll keep at it," Noel said. "Don't worry. You know, Mother, people do improve after they've had a stroke. I've read of lots of cases where an almost complete recovery has been made. Haven't you tried? Have you just been lying here day after day? You can blink, can't you? Blink once for yes and twice for no. Do you understand what you hear?"

The lids came down, slowly, as if fighting against a heavy counterweight. Once. And they remained steady.

"Does the doctor come regularly?"

Down and up again.

"Would you mind very much if you had a nurse looking after you? You heard Rosemary, didn't you? I think she needs to get away from here—maybe doing what I did. I went to a very reputable agency. There's no funny business about any of the places they send you to. Would you mind very much if she went away from here?"

There was no blinking this time, only the slow filling up of one eye, the same as yesterday. "All right," Noel said hastily. "It was only a thought. She probably wouldn't leave you anyway. She loves you very much. Now why don't you have a rest? You've done a lot this morning."

She picked up the pad and stared at the weird loops and squiggles on it. Was that meant to be "Rosemary"? And that one looked like "help." She put it down. It was like the ink blot test. One could read anything into it. She started a letter to Doug. It proved difficult. She'd been honest with him. She'd told him how she felt. What could she say now? "I still love him. I don't know why but my blood cries out for him. Whatever he is, whatever he's done." She stared out of the window. Doug would make a good husband. She didn't have that same certainty about Jonas.

Rosemary returned just after midday and Noel showed her the paper on which her mother had written. "I think with a little practice she'll be able to produce something that is readable."

"Aren't you the clever one? Do you imagine I've not tried that? It's always the same." She snatched the paper out of Noel's hand and screwed it up. "You can go now, your good deed done for the day."

Noel smiled at her mother. "See you later. We'll beat it yet."

Nicola had gone from names to menus and then to the telephone. She put the receiver down as Noel entered the room and put a neat tick beside a name halfway down her list. "Another said yes," she cried triumphantly.

"Great."

"I forgot to ask you. Do you want lunch? Only I usually just have an omelette and coffee and John eats in the kitchen. I won't have him in here tramping mud and straw all over the place. See Mrs. Cassell anyway. Tell her what you want."

"Could I borrow your car? I thought I might go into town. And if you want anything for tomorrow or Saturday I could get it for you."

"Have you got a licence for driving here?"

"Yes."

"I'm only thinking of the insurance." Nicola smiled with a hint of apology. "One must these days. Of course you can borrow it. You needn't bother about getting anything for me. I'll do it all by telephone. People are very good about delivering."

"The keys?"

"They'll be in the ignition. You will be careful, won't you? They drive on the other side in America, don't they?"

"I'll be careful."

It was ten miles into Elmsbury, the nearest town. She parked the car in a side street, locking it carefully. There were a lot of new shops, supermarkets mostly. She went into a couple and found they were way behind the American ones. There wasn't half the variety. The cafe she used to visit was still on the corner. She went inside only to retreat with speed. A juke box was going and it was crowded with teenagers, rowdy and noisy.

"The Ship" seemed to offer surroundings where she wouldn't stick out like a sore thumb. She went inside and sat at a corner table, running her eye down the menu. A prawn cocktail and then Weiner Schnitzel and a tossed green salad. "And a glass of white wine," she told the waiter as he turned away after taking her order.

She leaned back in her chair. The place was fairly full but the conversation was subdued and the tape churning out the standard orchestral background music was audible without intruding in any way.

She'd never been in "The Ship" before. A sign of the times. Now she was old enough and the time that afternoon was dragging by as if every second had lead feet.

The prawn cocktail was good. The Weiner Schnitzel even better. Or was it because she was so hungry? She had a sweet *and* cheese and biscuits. It was much better than an omelette with Nicola or eating with John. She ordered a Gaelic coffee to finish and lit a cigarette. The couple on the next table were just finishing too. They'd been talking about her for the last half hour if the constant glances were anything to go by but she was surprised when the man got up and said, "Excuse me, but you *are* Noel Clare, aren't you?"

She agreed she was a little warily.

"I'm Barry Neville. Perhaps Nicola has mentioned me to you. I'm a writer."

And he was a complete egoist too if she was any judge of character.

"I think perhaps your name might have cropped up in the conversation sometime," she said placidly. He was one of those attractive men who have to emphasise their good looks. His clothes were beautifully tailored, his dark wavy hair not too long and not too short, his smile a practised one of great charm showing perfect teeth. "May we join you for coffee? This is my wife, Marian." He held his hand out and she rose awkwardly, a painfully thin angular woman with greasy black hair cut close to her scalp in the square medieval style of a pageboy. "We were friends of Nicola's before she was married."

"The first time," Marian put in. She had a deep voice, almost mannish. She sat down in a jingle of sound. There were slave bangles on one arm, a charm bracelet on the other and at least six different kinds of beads dangling from her neck down to her waist. Her jumper was an indeterminate colour between green and yellow, her skirt made of some homespun cloth that couldn't have had a worse combination of colours. She had to have a brilliant mind if Mrs. Cassell's claim of smartness was to be believed.

"I understand you've been working in America," Barry said.

"Yes." She moved out of the way of the waiter who made an elaborate ritual of her coffee.

"I think I'll have one of those," Marian said, watching with greedy eyes.

The waiter glanced enquiringly at Barry who said, "I'll stick to black."

It came in a minute cup, hardly worth drinking. Marian put her tongue in the cream of her glass like a cat. "Delicious. Isn't it, Noel?"

"It certainly is." She was wondering how they knew she'd been working in America. She'd not told Nicola and whilst there'd been time during the day for Rosemary to have passed on the information to her there had surely been no opportunity for Nicola to pass it on further—unless she hadn't waited to tell John before issuing the invitations to dinner.

"Has Nicola phoned you this morning?"

"We've been here since nine—well not *here* precisely, but in Elmsbury. There's nothing wrong is there?" Barry put just the right amount of expression on his face, polite enquiry with a faint tinge of concern.

"No. I believe she'll be inviting you to dinner tomorrow, however."

"That *will* be nice. We'll be delighted to accept."

"Of course," Marian put in. "Nicola is always so hospitable. And while you're down here, Noel, you must come to us. Perhaps tonight?"

"I'm afraid I already have an engagement tonight and now if you'll excuse me." She caught the eye of the waiter. "My bill, please."

"You must allow me," Barry said. "No, really. Put the young lady's bill on mine."

"Very well. Thank you." She wasn't going to make a fight of it. "I'll see you tomorrow probably." She smiled at them both and made a graceful exit. She didn't like them and she didn't know why. They reminded her of birds of prey, the one the lure, the other the hungry vulture waiting to pick the bones. Stupid fancies. But there had been a hungry look in Marian's eyes, and a kind of anticipatory relish.

She glanced at her watch. How many hours left to kill? The hairdresser's. Always a good way of whiling away a couple of hours. She cashed a cheque first and then had her hair done in an elaborate style that probably wouldn't last two seconds in a high wind. She had no problem in deciding what to wear. White and gold, Indian style. She'd need something to go over it. A terylene mac was the only coat she'd brought with her. She bought a mohair stole, warm and soft and light to carry.

Nicola was still in her sitting room penning another list.

"Reporting safe delivery of one car," Noel said, putting her head round the door.

"Good. Enjoy yourself?" Nicola said absently and then looking up caught sight of her hair. "That's rather nice."

"Uhmm, yes. I thought so too. I won't be in for dinner, Nicola."

"Oh? Where are you going?"

"I don't know yet." She smiled vaguely and withdrew, half afraid Nicola would follow to ask who she was going with but Nicola was too immersed in her lists. She didn't ask that question until Noel came down again and then it was rather worse as there was an audience. John was there, neat and scrubbed, all traces of the farm dirt that offended Nicola banished from his person.

"I'm going with an old friend," she said.

Nicola accepted that but John's eyes darkened suspiciously. "What old friend?"

"No friend of yours."

The blare of a horn saved her from further questions. She picked up handbag and stole and made a rapid retreat. They'd probably recognise the car but there was nothing they could do about it to stop her going.

"Trouble?" Jonas asked as she ran out.

"Not really." She got into the car and he closed the door on her and went round to the other side. "How about you?"

"Christina was difficult—but don't worry. I'll sort it out." He started the car. "I have to go to London tomorrow and I'll probably be staying overnight. You'll still be here when I get back, won't you?"

"Haven't you heard? Nicola is throwing a party in my honour on Saturday. I'll be staying until then. And she *will* be disappointed. You were going to be invited to dinner tomorrow night as well. You're the most important man in the district! I wonder if she'll cancel it because you can't be there."

"I detect some kind of undercurrent running beneath that sarcasm. What else did she tell you?"

"Nothing very much. Except that she did imply you and she were *great* friends. What did she say now. . . ? 'A strange man, rude and overpowering—but there's something about him!'" She made a purring sound in her throat.

"Oh, there's quite definitely something about him."

"Did she say it like that?"

"No . . . the repeat was all mine." She laughed, watching the lines crinkle around his eyes. She didn't care what his relationship was with any other woman, not while she was with him.

The car sped through the dark lanes, the headlights pinning a fox, a rabbit and something she'd never seen in the road, a big barn owl that swooped down and then stood transfixed, the huge saucerlike eyes staring blindly into the light. Jonas had to cut the engine before it moved out of the way and took off, gliding up through the trees, a dark shadow against the moon.

"I missed the country," Noel murmured, as they moved off once more. "Talk how you will, there's something about the place where you were born that always has a pull on your heart. I suppose you feel the same way. Your family has lived here for generations. Why did Christina never give you a son, Jonas? You can't want the line to end with you."

"She didn't want children," he said slowly.

"There was always tomorrow—and then she had that accident."

"Did you ever love her?"

"She was beautiful—and she was rich. Those were the important things at that time. I was young. I couldn't bear to think of the manor going to anyone else. And I make no excuses. I still can't." He turned a corner a little too fast and the car rocked.

"No one can take it from you now, can they?" Noel said cautiously.

His mouth was set in a hard line. "It will be over my dead body."

Noel pulled her stole around her tightly. Could Christina strip him of his money? Had she threatened to try? Was that what being difficult meant?

"I'll be seeing my solicitors tomorrow," Jonas said abruptly and he turned his head as if he'd read her thoughts. "Don't worry. I won't let any of it touch you. Christina will recognise the inevitable and listen to reason. Now let's talk about something different. Are you hungry?"

"Starving," she said promptly. "And I had a massive lunch too but Mrs. Cassell ruined my breakfast for me and Rosemary spoiled my dinner last night so I have a lot to make up. Where are you taking me?"

"How would you like to go down to the coast? There's a pub I know and it will be quiet at this time of the year."

"Sounds fine."

She didn't think of the lateness of the hour in coming back. Now that she was with him time ceased to exist.

The pub was on the shingle in a tiny village. They ate overlooking the sea, a placid one for November, with the moon turning the waves to silver.

They were the only ones in the dining room and they had to wait as their meal was started from scratch. It didn't matter. Nothing mattered. He told her she was beautiful and it was as though no one had ever told her that before. He touched her hand and her skin tingled, retaining the touch until the next time their hands met and held. She drank a lot and ate a lot and talked a lot and he watched her and listened, a half smile on his face. "I'm ten years older than you," he said once, abruptly, and she laughed at him. "You'll bless that ten years. You'll know how to hold me."

The moon climbed higher and they walked

out on to the shingle to the sand, their foot-prints leaving a trail to the water's edge and there he kissed her again, the wind whipping her hair from its precarious setting and sending it flying about her face. He smoothed it back holding her face in his cupped hands and there was no longer any laughter in his face. It was dark and remote and her heart almost stopped beating. If she should ever lose him now.

A wave, stronger than the rest, spilled out over their feet and he jumped back, pulling her away, the laughter back in his eyes. "We must go. This isn't the time for waiting for the dawn." And he took her hand, running back along the beach until she was breathless and gasping. "Into the car. Take those shoes off." He turned the heater full on and they travelled back in a cocoon of warm air. "Happy?" he asked.

She nodded, curled up in the seat. "But I'm so sleepy. I can hardly keep my eyes open."

"It will be after three when we get back."

That was almost as good as a douche of cold water. "John will have locked me out," she said with conviction.

Jonas was silent for a moment, then he said,

"You can go to 'The Ship.' They'll put you up for the night."

She reached slowly for a cigarette and his voice was gentle and amused. "It's not a proposition. No one will be able to put a label on you for staying there."

She blushed and hoped the darkness would hide it. She'd not blushed for years. "It's just that I know what they'll think."

"Yes," he said dryly. "Never let other people rule your life, Noel."

"Just you?"

"Yes. Just me." He reached over and took her hand. "I'll stop at the next call box and fix it up."

It was just before three when he pulled up the car outside "The Ship." There was a night porter on duty and Jonas handed her over. "This is Miss Clare, Sam. Look after her." She was ready to fall asleep on the hardest couch. She smiled at him sleepily. "I'll see you."

"That you will." He touched her hand and then he had gone. She followed the porter up the stairs, barely taking in the room. She was asleep within a second of putting her head on the pillow and she didn't open her eyes again until a knock at the door brought her dimly to the surface.

"Sleepyhead."

She was suddenly very wide awake. "Jonas!"

"I brought you some clothes. You can't very well walk out of here in that sari outfit. I can't stop." He put down a bag from one of Elmsbury's most expensive dress shops and smiled down at her. "If you meet any trouble from John come back here. I'll find you."

"All right."

He placed a finger on her lips. "Keep them for me," and then he was gone again. She sat up. A tea tray on the table. She felt the pot. Stone cold. Wondering if the maid had tried very hard to wake her she rang for room service and ordered coffee and toast.

It arrived when she was in the bathroom. She came out with the towel wrapped around her and tipped the maid. It was almost ten. It was after eleven when she left the room.

Jonas had bought her a dress and coat in matching materials of jade and midnight. The smart effect was spoiled by her sand-stained gold slippers but she blessed him for the thought. The foyer was crowded. In sari and stole a lot of eyebrows would have been raised.

She found Jonas had attended to the bill too and a taxi was ready for her, also arranged. He dropped her at the farm and when she tried to pay him said the hotel had fixed it.

She went in by the back door and Mrs. Cassell regarded her grimly. "No Cinderella act for you, I see."

"What's the temperature? Boiling over or freezing point?"

"There were words last night," Mrs. Cassell said darkly. "But nothing this morning; everyone is carefully avoiding any mention of you at all—at least in our presence. Where have you been?"

"It was late and I was afraid John would have either locked me out or be waiting with a shotgun. I stayed at 'The Ship'."

"Alone, I hope?"

"Of course alone."

"And bought a new outfit too?"

"Now, Mrs. Cassell, you've not made an inventory of my clothes, have you?"

"I know that bag. Sarah Jane. She's expensive. Leave that here. Dear me." She pulled out the sari. "What have you been doing in this? Paddling? I'll wash it for you. Take those shoes off too—though I think they're ruined."

"You're an angel to me, Mrs. Cassell. I don't know what I've done to deserve it." She slipped off the shoes and managed to reach her room without bumping into anyone but Sharon.

She changed into slacks and sweater and went into her mother's room. She was alone. "We'll have another practice, shall we?" Noel said, putting the pad on the counterpane and placing the pen in her mother's hand again.

It was just the same. Meaningless scrawls and squiggles. "Never mind," Noel said cheerfully when the sheet had been filled. "It will come." She perched on the window seat and started telling her mother about America, drawing pictures of Boston and New York, California and Florida—all the places she'd seen—the people she'd met and worked for.

Nicola broke it up. She pushed the door open and said, "I thought I heard your voice. Did you enjoy yourself last night?"

"Very much."

"Good." Nicola dismissed it with that and went on to talk about the party, leaving Noel considerably disconcerted but naturally reluctant to reintroduce the topic herself. "Jonas unfortunately won't be able to make it tonight," Nicola went on. "Christina tells me that he's in London."

They couldn't have recognised the car. Maybe they even thought she'd been in early and gone straight to bed. What was the matter with her? Had she wanted the excitement of a full scale row?

Even Rosemary avoided her eyes when they met at lunch. Nicola had insisted they have it together to go over everything she had arranged. Thirty-eight people had accepted her invitation. "And I've invited Fred Garnett," Nicola said to Noel. "John tells me you used to be friends. I asked him to dinner tonight too. He sounded delighted at the opportunity of seeing you again."

Noel glanced up and met the malicious amusement on Rosemary's face. "What about a man for Rosemary?" she said. "You've surely not left her out?"

"Well—" Nicola hesitated, searching for words and Rosemary jumped in coldly, "I don't need a man. The world won't come to an end if there's an odd number at the table."

"Christina will be on her own," Nicola put in placatingly. "That is, Jonas won't be with her. Dr. Shepherd will be bringing her with Lady Valerie."

"Why isn't Jonas coming? I would have thought nothing would keep him away." The sidelong glance Rosemary gave Noel was provocative.

"He's in London," Nicola said hastily. "Now, Rosemary—what are you wearing?"

"If you'll excuse me . . ." Noel rose. "I'll exercise Tempest unless there's something you want me to do, Nicola?"

"No, no. Everything is organised."

It was really very odd Noel thought as she rode on Tempest out to the ridge. Nicola's affability worried her. And why should it?

She reigned in, bending down to pat Tempest's neck and something zipped past her ear, followed by a dull popping report.

She didn't wait for a repetition. Digging her heels into Tempest's flanks she took off like a rocket and didn't stop until she reached the cover of the trees.

Someone had fired a shot at her? Deliberately? She crossed the river at a more sober pace, reasonably certain that she was now well out of range, and went up to the tower.

Leaving Tempest to graze in the grassy forecourt she mounted the crumbling steps that went spiralling up to the open sky. The tower had been rebuilt in Napoleonic times when a constant watch had been kept for any signs of an invading French army. It had been the west tower of a castle built in Norman times but nothing much of the castle remained; steps, a wall here and there, part of a room, a narrow parapet, slitted windows, what might have been a fireplace and enough fallen stone to build an office block.

The place was dangerous. There were warning notices all over the place but people ignored them. It was an attraction. The huge tower, the ruins, the drawbridge and the grassed moat with the long stretch of turf beyond crying out for picnics to be taken on it. But that was in the summer. There were no picnickers now.

Noel climbed to the top, very conscious of how alone she was. If someone with a rifle was stalking her it would be easy enough to pick her off without anyone being any the wiser.

She had a fantastic view. The fields and meadows, trees and straight hedges and walls. The patchwork scene of England. A toy tractor moved across a brown field, two men digging a hole looked like stiff marionettes, a thin trickle of smoke came from the farm chimneys, a figure on horseback travelled across the long meadow. It was much too far away for her to make out who it was. She waited for them to turn into the road but a careless movement sent her foot on a piece of stone that gave way beneath her. She slipped and fell down half a dozen of the steps before the edge of the outer wall brought her up short.

Considerably white of face she looked at the drop on the other side. The familiar vertigo overtook her. She was all right looking at the view but that straight plunge down into the tower always had the effect of paralysing her. By the time she'd infused some stiffener into her trembling limbs the figure on horseback had gone.

To the farm? Or through the trees to the village? But Christina couldn't ride. She could drive a car though.

She climbed down shakily. She'd gashed her arm and the blood was soaking into the sleeve of her sweater. Was she going to scream murder because someone had taken a pot shot at her? It could have been meant to frighten her, to scare her off. Rosemary, for instance. Or John.

Or it could simply have been an accident. Someone after rabbits.

She had nothing with which to bind the gash and climbing on Tempest again she went back to the farm as fast as Tempest could make it. If someone was lying in wait she wasn't going to present them with a good target.

One of the men was in the stables filling the troughs. She slid off Tempest awkwardly. Her arm was beginning to hurt. "Can you see to Tempest? I've had a bit of an accident?"

"Surely." He came over, his eyes widening. "That looks bad."

"The blood makes it look worse. It's not as fearsome as all that. Has anyone else been out? I thought I saw someone riding across the meadow."

"Not from here. At least I don't think so. You ought to get the doctor to see to that, Miss."

Nicola agreed with him. She bumped into Noel coming in and shrieked. Before Noel could do anything about it she had bundled her into the car and was driving her to Dr. Shepherd's.

"You've got to be careful. Tetanus, you know. People can die of that."

Dr. Shepherd lived on the edge of the village in a solid, substantial house that looked more like a vicarage than a doctor's residence. Noel had known him since her childhood. He had seen her though mumps and measles, whooping cough, a broken leg, various strains and sprains and a suspected fracture. "I might have known you wouldn't be back long before paying me a visit," he said resignedly. "What have you done this time?"

"I fell."

"Oh yes?" He pushed up the sleeve of her sweater and began to clean the wound. It stretched from her elbow almost down to her wrist and was now exceedingly painful. She yelped.

"Where's your stiff upper lip?" he said without sympathy.

"I think I must have left it at home." She gloomily surveyed her arm. "It's going to need stitches, isn't it?"

"A few."

It didn't feel like a few. He bandaged it and gave her a tetanus injection and then sent them on their way, saying he was looking forward to his dinner that night.

84

"I can't think why he and Lady Valerie don't get married," Nicola remarked.

"What?" Noel couldn't imagine it. Lady Valerie, so cultured and elegant, and the blunt, balding Dr. Shepherd with his well worn clothes that didn't seem to have changed since she'd last seen him.

"They're very fond of one another and they're both free. It's very hard for Christina to have her mother-in-law living with them all the time. Not that there's any friction between them but Jonas is very fond of his mother and he tends to see things her way instead of his wife's."

Nicola drove fast and not very well and she didn't seem to know what gears were for.

Noel sat with her feet braced against the floor of the car. "Do you mean they quarrel?"

"What married couple doesn't?" Nicola said flippantly. "But Christina's looking forward to being alone with Jonas for a change."

"Oh? She's planning on making the doctor propose tonight?"

Nicola laughed. "I don't know about that but I do know she and Jonas are going on a cruise. Christina plans to make it a second honeymoon. Apparently she's seen a new doctor and he thinks there's a chance she might be able to have a child. They're very excited about it, of course. Jonas desperately wants a son and if Christina can pull it off she'll make him the happiest man in Henton."

Noel heard her voice from a long way off. "When do they go?"

"Next week. Tuesday I think. Jonas has gone to London to fix all the last-minute details. There are an awful lot of arrangements to be made whenever he goes away of course—such a busy man. He told Christina he might not even get back for the party."

"That would be a pity." She felt numb. It wasn't true. It couldn't be true. A second honeymoon? Had last night been a lie? Or was Christina preparing for a fight?

4

IT was going to be a fight. Noel knew it the moment she laid her hand in Christina's and offered the conventional greeting.

There was awareness in Christina's eyes, the same awareness of a prize fighter measuring up his opponent in the opposite corner—and she was still very beautiful. It was disconcerting—and at the same time exhilarating. Christina wasn't going to play on her disability. There was too much pride in her, the pride of a woman who had always dictated her own terms and had never known defeat.

She smiled at Noel, a smile that was both imperious and gracious; the lady of the manor being kind to the scullery maid. Her voice was low and sweet. "At last we meet! I've heard so much about you—from one source or another. How are you, Noel? Oh? You've had an accident?" Her quick eyes caught sight of the bandage that was meant to be concealed under the long flowing sleeve of Noel's gown.

"It's nothing. A scratch."

"A scratch indeed," Nicola commented scornfully. "Thirteen stitches she had in there."

"Oh dear. I hope you're not superstitious." Christina's eyes were blue, innocent and ingenuous, but her hair was red, a rich glowing beacon shouting beware.

"Not at all," Noel said lightly.

The smile returned to Christina's face. She said smoothly, "It takes a wise woman to know when her luck has run out. The first pointer should never be ignored." She leaned up as Nicola relieved her of her fur jacket. "Thank you, darling." She was wearing a low cut gown of metallic thread that glittered as she moved. It covered her legs completely but the tips of pale blue satin slippers peeped out from beneath it. Apart from the fact that she was in a wheelchair she looked perfectly normal, as if she could stand and walk away from it if she chose. And maybe get on a horse and use a rifle too?

Noel hesitated and instead of following them into Nicola's sitting room where John was dispensing drinks, she turned and went into the little room he used as his office. His rifle was in the long cupboard, together with a shot gun, propped carelessly in the corner. She picked it up and held it to her nose, sniffing tentatively. It smelt of oil, as if it had been cleaned not long ago.

"What on earth are you doing?" Rosemary exclaimed behind her.

Noel jumped violently but she managed to smile as she turned round. "Nothing," she said airily, and put the rifle down. "When did John last go out shooting?"

"Why don't you ask him?" Rosemary said maliciously.

"You think I won't?" Noel raised her eyebrows. "How about you, Rosemary?"

"Now I wonder what exactly is running through that mind of yours now," Rosemary said musingly, leaning against the wall and regarding Noel through half-closed eyes. "Can it be that you imagine we want to get rid of you? Does that bandage on your arm hide the mark of an assassin's bullet? But surely Dr. Shepherd would have mentioned that. He said it was a cut. You'd scraped your arm against something sharp."

"So you went to the trouble of asking him." Noel's tone matched her sister's in its silken softness. "I wouldn't have thought you would show so much concern."

"Oh, but I feel for you. I do, I do." Rosemary pushed herself upright. "I came to tell you that your swain has arrived, panting eagerly at the prospect of seeing you. No, not Jonas," she added softly. "Fred! He obviously hasn't heard of last night yet but no doubt the word will get around. Christina knows. I doubt if you'll hold your head up so high when she's finished with you." She smiled and slipped from the room and rather slowly Noel followed her, to be buttonholed at once by Fred.

He had grown a flourishing moustache and put on a couple of stones in her absence but he was just the same naïve young boy, stammering a little in his eagerness to talk to her, his ruddy face shining as he at once started detailing his achievements of the years to make it quite obvious he was now a man of substance, worthy of her attention.

She stood pinned against the wall until Lady Valerie rescued her by joining them.

Noel was very fond of Lady Valerie who had taken their Sunday School class for many years, and her smile was warm. "Lady Valerie!"

"Noel, my dear. How are you?" She was a small woman radiating great charm and she took Noel's proffered hand in both her own. "You look a little pale."

"Maybe she's been having too many late nights." Wielding her wheelchair with skilful dexterity, Christina rolled between them.

"The young can stand a great many late nights." Lady Valerie smiled. "You look charming, Noel I like that dress."

"From Sarah Jane's, is it?" Christina asked sweetly.

Noel kept her face blank but it was an effort. "New York, actually. One of the great bargain basement offers."

"Noel! Darling! How lovely you look."

She reeled back from the blast of booze-laden breath. The Nevilles were late but obviously, in Barry's case at least, they had no catching up to do.

"Now we're all here I think we might start eating," Nicola said gaily. "Come on, everybody."

Mrs. Cassell and Sharon had made a work of art of the table. It looked beautiful. And the meal was one that commanded praise. Nicola accepted the compliments complacently, as if she alone were responsible.

Noel was sitting next to Fred and opposite

Christina. The conversation was general until Christina put down her cheese knife and, looking directly at Noel, asked abruptly if she liked the Americans.

"Very much," Noel said, on the alert at once. Christina had discarded the gloves and was getting down to the serious business of the evening.

"There are many qualities about the Americans which one has to admire. Others are not so admirable," she said pensively.

"You're probably right," Noel agreed affably.

"Living so long with them you must have acquired some of their characteristics."

"Oh?" Noel wondered what on earth Christina was leading up to. Lady Valerie was looking at her daughter-in-law with a shade of apprehension on her face.

"I've not met any Americans," Christina said, glancing round the table, demanding, and holding, the attention of them all. "But of course I know all about Adele Beaton. She murdered to get what she wanted."

"She did nothing of the sort," Lady Valerie put in with some asperity.

"Maybe she didn't do the actual deed but she

was the cause of Lydia's death." Christina turned her wide-eyed gaze on Lady Valerie. "What must that poor woman have felt when her husband brought his mistress into his own home, conferring on her all the rights and privileges of a wife, commanding the servants to do her bidding and disregard the orders of his lawful wife? She was treated like an outcast in her own home, banished to a suite of rooms at the top of the house. Can you wonder that she took her own life? There was no alternative; her money had gone, squandered by her husband, her looks had faded, she had no family to turn to. What did the future hold but more humiliation and shame? Even in this day and age I think Lydia would have chosen to die. She loved her husband very much. There has always been a fatal attraction about the Fenton men."

Noel picked up an apple. The knife in her hand flashed in the light as she wielded it, her fingers graceful and rock steady. She didn't intend to be provoked into any part of this but Christina threw the challenge right at her. "What do you think Lydia would do if James Fenton brought his mistress to live under her nose and it happened now—this week perhaps?"

"Ancient history always did bore me. I see no point in resurrecting the past," she said without raising her eyes from the apple.

"But history has a habit of repeating itself. Don't you agree?"

Noel glanced up, meeting Christina's apparently innocent gaze calmly. "Does history reveal that Lydia made an attempt on Adele's life before taking her own?"

Christina blinked. For a moment Noel thought she had scored a bull's eye but then she smiled. "Lydia would never have done that. She was no savage; she had been gently reared. Adele was the one who resorted to violence. She would have done anything to get what she wanted."

"You talk as if you knew her personally," Fred said, his brow creasing worriedly. He was probably the only one around the table who didn't know what Christina was getting at but he did sense something was wrong. "What does the past matter? It couldn't happen like that nowadays. People wouldn't allow it and if you ask me Lydia sounds a pretty spineless character. She should have sent that hussy packing right at the start."

Christina leaned forward across the table and

said earnestly, "You're so right, Frederick. She was weak. I would never take that way out. Never! Any young madam trying to take my husband away from me would have to murder me herself. I wouldn't do the job for her."

"You wouldn't have to," Noel put in tartly, unable to resist the temptation. "These days there's a very simple solution. It's called divorce. Maybe you've heard of it. Several thousand people take advantage of it each year and it's vastly superior to taking the law into your own hands and risking a life sentence for murder."

Christina drew back. There was nothing in her eyes now but a dark enmity. "There will never be a divorce. If you take Jonas it will be over my dead body."

There it was. Right out into the open. The flatness of Christina's statement hung in the air. No one spoke. No one even moved. Not until Noel got to her feet. "So be it," she said quietly and turned and left the room.

She was to regret those words. In fact, even before she had reached her own bedroom she was regretting them. It was what Christina had wanted. A public declaration—a throwing down of the gauntlet. What did she hope to gain by it? The moral indignation of John rising to the fore to throw her out again? The sympathy of her friends to present a solid front of disapproval which would drive her away, shamed and humiliated because she had made the mistake of falling in love with a married man?

She lay on the bed without turning on the light. Nicola would handle John. She didn't have to worry about that. And to be an outcast, snubbed and derided by people who had been her friends? It would hurt. People's sympathies would inevitably go to Christina. The beautiful crippled wife in her wheelchair. She should be ashamed. She wondered why she was not; why she couldn't feel sorry for Christina. What kind of girl could plan to deprive a crippled woman of her husband? She was worse than Adele.

She heard voices, a car engine, subdued farewells. Christina had certainly broken up that dinner party.

Her door was burst open without warning. John! It had to be John.

He switched on the light and advanced to the foot of the bed, his hands clenched, a vein prominently throbbing in his forehead.

Noel didn't move.

"You little slut," he said in a low thick voice.

96

"You couldn't wait a moment. Get out of here. Now . . . this instant, before I forget myself and give you the hiding you should have had seven years ago."

"Go away, John," Noel said wearily.

"I mean it."

"And so do I." She slid off the bed and stood up, reaching for the long zip in her dress. "I'm going to bed."

Maybe it was her indifference to his threat, maybe the calm assumption that he would have to leave as she started to undress. Whatever it was it tipped the balance and John bounded forward, his face contorted with anger. "You dirty, filthy hussy."

She had an instant's awareness but it was too late; her hands were behind her, she was wide open to attack and John's blow landed with such force she was sent halfway across the room to land sprawled across the carpet.

For a moment she thought she'd been blinded. Everything went black and then as the mists cleared she heard Nicola screaming at John. The words didn't make sense. She shook her head, feeling sick and dizzy, and slowly and laboriously got to her feet.

John was turned away from her. He was still

furiously angry. Every line of his body was taut with his fury. "All right she can stay," he shouted. "But don't expect me to apologise. There's not a man nor woman in Henton who would blame me for what I've done. Bringing shame on us like that and not even caring what people think of us."

Noel's knees buckled under her. She groped for the bed and sat down. She couldn't see out of her left eye. She put a hand to her face and felt the rapidly rising swelling on her cheekbone.

"You're going to have a beautiful black eye," Nicola said quietly. "Lie down. I'll bathe it for you."

She was back in a moment and leaving Noel holding the cold flannel against her eye, she said, "I'm sorry. I had no idea he could be so violent."

"I suppose I'm lucky you arrived when you did. My mother stopped him last time."

"Last time?"

"Oh, you surely know why I was sent away now. John put two and two together and made about seventy-five out of it."

"So there was nothing in it?"

Noel squinted at her. "You sound almost disappointed. I was only a kid."

"But you're not now, are you?"

Noel dropped the flannel in the cold water and slowly squeezed it out. "No, I'm not," she said briefly.

"You've got Christina worried. What are you going to do?"

"Nothing."

"Oh, come now. I wasn't born yesterday and you're too sure of yourself by far. What's going on?"

"Nothing."

"Nothing, nothing, nothing! Is that all you say? At least tell me one thing—are you going to be here until Saturday?"

Noel removed the flannel, blinking at Nicola in sheer astonishment. "You're not still holding your party?"

"Why not? Or are you afraid to show your face?" She laughed at Noel's expression. "All right. You'd never admit it. So you think people won't come? But they will. Curiosity will bring them at the gallop."

"Actually I was thinking of Christina. She must have a lot of friends."

"Christina won't repeat tonight's performance.

She was very apologetic about it. You really shouldn't have taunted her, Noel. It was a cruel thing to do."

"I? Taunted her?"

"You deny it?" Nicola laughed. "I suppose you didn't know what you were doing! What it is to be young and beautiful . . . and so sure of one's self." She picked up the bowl of water, pausing at the doorway. "What will you do if Jonas does nothing about a divorce?"

"You think that's likely?"

"*You* don't—that's obvious—but don't make the mistake of underestimating Christina. She has coped with many a crisis in the past." There was more than a hint of maliciousness in Nicola's smile. "You'll not find it as easy as you expect."

She closed the door softly behind her and Noel groaned. Where was this confidence, this assurance that people saw in her? She didn't feel at all sure of herself. Or of Jonas. She only knew that she loved him and it was a force over which she had not the slightest control.

She went over to the mirror and winced at the sight. Maybe it would be better tomorrow.

But it wasn't. She could just about open her eye and use it, but it was bloodshot, the area around it black and blue. And she hadn't had the forethought to bring her sunglasses. Who would have thought she'd need them in November?

Nicola lent her some huge round ones that virtually masked half her face. "How are you going to explain it?" she asked.

"Isn't it usual to say you walked into a door?"

"You could *say* it," Nicola said doubtfully. "You'll keep out of John's way today, won't you?"

"I've not exactly been courting his company since I arrived and last night hasn't exactly given me the incentive to change my habits."

She went in to see her mother but Rosemary was washing her and she didn't stay, going back just before lunch when Rosemary had gone down for her tray.

"I've had an idea," she said cheerfully. "Look." She showed her mother what she'd done, writing out the alphabet on top of her pad. "Now you just drop your finger as I move it along. Is there anything you want?"

The finger dropped on "g".

"Fine, fine." Noel wrote it down. It was followed by "o". She had a feeling what was coming then and her pencil faltered as it spelled out, "Go away."

"You too?" she whispered. But her mother hadn't finished. 'Danger," she spelled out. "R—"

"What are you doing now?" Rosemary demanded, coming in with a loaded tray. She dropped it on the chair and snatched at the paper but Noel made no attempt to keep it from her.

She watched her read it, expecting the same reaction as before but Rosemary didn't screw it up.

"So go on," she said, putting it down in front of her mother. "What is it going to be? 'Rosemary hates you?' But my dear sister already knows that. Go on. What's stopping you?"

Noel stared at her mother who made no attempt to drop her finger on one of the letters. "Was that what you were going to say?" she asked slowly.

Her mother closed her eyes but didn't open them again and Noel stared at her, frustrated and uncertain. Could her mother be afraid of Rosemary?

"There was a call for you this morning," Rosemary said. "I left a message on the pad.

Christina wanted you to go round for lunch. She said she had something very important to discuss with you. She talked to Jonas this morning." She picked up a bowl of soup from the tray and whisked a napkin round her mother's neck. "Well? Aren't you going? I thought you'd rush off there."

"Do you truly hate me, Rosemary. Would you hurt me if you could?"

Rosemary stared at her and then her eyes dropped. "You should never have come back," she muttered.

"Someone took a shot at me yesterday."

"I gathered that. You think it was me?"

"Can you shoot?"

"Not well enough to take chances. I assume you don't imagine your life was in danger?"

"I would feel a lot happier if I could be sure of that."

Rosemary uttered a short laugh. "I'm not the one to dispel your uncertainty. I'll tell you something though. John did clean his rifle yesterday. Did you notice that when you were sniffing it?"

"You mean John had been using it?"

"It figures. Did you ask him if he took a shot at you? And get your answer?" She smiled without humour. "A pity Nicola interrupted last night. Maybe next time she won't be around."

"There won't be a next time." Noel swung on her heel. Was it suspicious that Rosemary had tried to throw the blame on John?

She went downstairs to the kitchen, pausing with her hand on the door handle as she heard the rumble of John's voice.

Nicola had already eaten her omelette and was nowhere to be seen. Noel picked an apple out of the bowl and paused at the pad by the telephone.

Rosemary had certainly left a message. "Christina wants to see you. Right away. She'll give you lunch."

Noel left it on the pad and tried the kitchen again. It sounded quiet so she pushed the door open and saw Sharon and Mrs. Cassell were in the middle of their own meal.

"I'm hungry," she said plaintively.

"But I thought you were going over to the manor for lunch." Mrs. Cassell got to her feet hurriedly. "I can fix you a salad."

Noel gazed at the succulent pork chops on the plates, the apple sauce, the roast potatoes, the garden peas and glazed carrots. "A salad will be fine," she said with an effort. "But I'll make it. You get on with your own lunch."

"No, no. It will only take a minute. You'll eat here with us?"

"Why not?" She sat down and smiled at Sharon, who stared at her sullenly. "I didn't take it."

"Hush now," Mrs. Cassell said soothingly. "Noel wouldn't be accusing you."

"Take what?" Noel said blankly. Had someone seen Sharon going through her case and bag? But she'd not mentioned the missing envelope to anyone.

"No one's taken anything." Mrs. Cassell deftly sliced some tomatoes. "What use would an itsy bitsy fruit knife be to anyone? It's just been mislaid. We'll look through the pig bin afterwards. That's where it'll be. It's happened before. I lost my potato peeler that way."

"That Mrs. Clare practically said I'd taken it."

"She was upset. It's one of a set. Her and her sets." Mrs. Cassell slid the salad in front of Noel and returned to her own meal. "You know what she is like. Possessions are important to a woman like that. She measures her success by them. Now forget about it. How did the meal go last night, Noel?"

"Very well. You could get a job anywhere in this district—but you know that, don't you? Lady Valerie asked Nichola for your recipe of that praline sweet and Dr. Shepherd had two helpings of the pavlova."

Mrs. Cassell smiled, gratified, but said, "I wondered if something had gone wrong. They went very early."

So she hadn't heard. "Well . . ." Noel glanced at Sharon eating stolidly with her head down. "Christina announced that I'd marry Jonas over her dead body and it rather put a stop to any general conversation."

"Oh dear!" Mrs. Cassell stared, her knife and fork poised in mid-air.

"Exactly."

"Is that what you want?"

"Christina dead?" Noel said, raising her brows high.

"No, silly. To marry Jonas."

"More than anything," Noel said quietly.

Mrs. Cassell shook her head regretfully. "You'd have done better to forget him."

"I tried. Believe me I tried."

"Are you afraid of Christina?"

Noel pushed her plate away. "Because I didn't jump to her command? I'll go and see her but I won't eat with her."

"You'll have some pie?"

She nodded and Mrs. Cassell cut three generous helpings and poured cream over them from a bright yellow jug.

"I wouldn't go if I was you," Sharon said unexpectedly. "That Mrs. Fenton is smart. You can blame her for that black eye you're hiding behind those dark glasses."

"What do you mean?" Noel said, startled both at Sharon's intervention and the venom in her voice.

"She was talking to him. I saw her, and I saw John's face. A clever woman can make John do anything. He can't see beyond the end of his nose . . . ever." She dug her spoon into the apple pie so hard the cream splattered.

"Explain yourself," Mrs. Cassell said sharply.

Sharon looked up, surprised. "What's there to explain? She wants Noel out of the way. Last night was her first try. Today will be her second."

Or maybe the third. Noel finished her pie pensively. Maybe Christina would try the obvious today. Without any witnesses she could allow her pride to slip and throw herself on Noel's mercy.

She walked over to the manor, aware of a reluctance that hadn't been helped by Sharon's parting words. "If you've got to go, be careful. She didn't come out with all that guff about Adele for nothing."

Sharon knew far more than she was saying. How had she known that Adele had been brought up, for instance? And that the dark glasses hid a black eye? And for that matter, how did she know the story of Adele? It wasn't talked about all that much in general conversation.

The manor lay on a slight rise, shrouded by the trees, a half-timbered house that sprawled untidily, the various extensions added without apparent thought for style of conformity.

Noel approached from the rear and circled around, the reluctance joined with an unease that grew stronger with every passing moment. The front door stood open. She stood on the threshold and rang the bell but no one came.

The hall was large and spacious. Her footsteps echoed hollowly on the black and white marble tiles that some long dead Fenton had brought from Italy.

"Christina?" Her voice echoed too. She opened the doors, glancing in each room, a strong mistrust telling her to run from this house. A table was set for two in a small room at the back of the house, half a grapefruit with a cherry on the top in each place. In the kitchen the aroma of some kind of casserole hit her as she opened the door. Coffee bubbled in a percolator and there was a tray set out with a cheese board and a variety of biscuits.

She came back into the hall, looking up at the stairs which rose in a T-junction, balustrades running along the long gallery.

Slowly, she mounted, her eyes on the portrait of Christina that hung at the top of the stairs. She wore an evening gown in a deep sapphire colour and she was smiling. She looked full of life, beautiful and provocative.

"It's good, isn't it?" Christina said in a mocking voice. "I could walk then."

Noel turned.

Christina was at the end of the gallery, half hidden in the shadows. "Come and see Lydia," she said. "She was almost pretty once."

Noel walked past the line of portraits and stood silently before the one Christina indicated. Lydia must have been very young when she was married. She looked scarcely out of her teens, a timid fair-haired girl of ethereal fragility.

"And this is Adele." Christina spun her chair round and leaning forward touched a switch. A light sprung out over a recess and Noel caught her breath. If Christina's portrait had been life-like this one was more than life. The vitality of the girl sprang out to hit at the senses. Blacker than black hair, tumbling down over her shoulders, large brilliant eyes and a curved mouth that was an invitation in itself. There were jewels at her throat and ears but they were secondary. The eyes demanded and held the gaze. "It was said she could hold people spell-bound," Christina said matter of factly. "No one could resist her. Even her own sex fell over themselves to do what she wanted. Do you think she could have hypnotised Lydia to kill herself?"

"It's impossible to hypnotise anyone into doing anything against their natural instincts," Noel said shortly.

"I've heard that said but who knows what a person's natural instincts are? Yours for instance? I thought you weren't going to accept my invitation. Are you nervous?"

"Should I be?"

"You were hurt yesterday. An accident?"

"Do you mean my arm? Or this?" She removed the glasses. "I understand you were responsible for John's rush of blood to the head."

"Dear me." Christina's smile was bland. "It's surprising what a few well-chosen words can do. Would Jonas have you, do you think, if you weren't quite so lovely to look at? He found he couldn't love a cripple."

"What are you getting at?" Noel said in a hard voice.

"Do you know what I told John?"

"No. And I don't think I want to know either."

"I'm surprised you got off with a black eye. Have you thought what a man like John could do if he really lost control?"

"He won't touch me again."

"I wouldn't be too sure of that. I could have another little talk with him."

"It won't work, Christina. Even if you do scare me off Jonas will find me."

"Not if you don't want to be found." She put her hand on the balustrade. "Did you know this was where Lydia killed herself? She went head first on that marble floor."

"You certainly have a fixation about that marriage."

"Not at all. It's a lesson and I intend to profit by it. Didn't you wonder why you found no one around downstairs? There are no witnesses; Lady Valerie is out for the day, I gave the servants the afternoon off and Jonas, of course, is in London."

"A number of people know I'm here."

Christina gave a crow of laughter. "You think I'm going to kill you? No, no. It's the other way around. That was what the talk last night was leading up to. Didn't you realise that? You've got a choice. Either you give me your promise that you'll go away and leave Jonas to me or I'll kill myself and you'll be had up for my murder."

5

NOEL took a step away from Christina. She couldn't mean it. She had to be bluffing. "You're crazy," she said flatly.

"Perhaps, but I mean it, Noel. Either way you lose him but you'll have a far better life with your American boyfriend than you would have behind bars."

"I don't believe you'd do it."

"No one else would either. Everyone knows how I feel about life. I'd never give it up voluntarily."

"I'm calling your bluff. Go ahead."

"And have you pull me back? I'll wait until you're out of this house. You might hear the thud. Do you think it will make much of a noise?" She smiled again, mockingly confident.

"I'm going to call Nicola and ask her to stay with you," Noel said grimly.

"You'll be too late."

"So I'll be too late." She turned her back on Christina but every nerve shrieked at her to look back, ready to spring. Every step took her further out of reach. Every step made her closer to being a murderer.

At the head of the stairs she turned her head. Christina hadn't moved. She wouldn't, of course. Who would kill herself for such a reason? It had been a try on. Like last night.

She wanted to run down the stairs, to run from the house. Why hadn't she followed that first impulse when she had entered?

"I hope you rot in hell," Christina screamed at her suddenly. "Have you no feeling? Don't you care about anyone else but yourself? Will you be able to sleep at night knowing you've caused the death of a cripple?"

She was mad enough. Crazy enough.

Noel stopped. She couldn't walk away. No one could. "Very well," she said heavily. "I'll go back to America. I won't see Jonas again."

"Swear it. Swear it on your life."

"On my life . . . I swear it." She closed her eyes, the sting of tears burning behind the lids. She put the dark glasses back on and Christina became a figure in the shadows again.

"You're to leave right away," she commanded. "If you don't keep your promise you know what will happen. I've left a letter. If I die it goes straight to the police and Jonas will be implicated too. I'll make sure of that."

"You've made your point. You needn't dress it up." She went down the stairs, crossing the marble floor to the front door. A pale sun was shining. She paused outside, angry with herself for not having the courage to hold out. It had been a cheap trick to get rid of her and she was a fool to allow herself to be influenced by it.

She could go back now, phone Nicola to come over and tell Christina what she could do with her threat the minute someone was there to bear witness and stop her doing anything stupid.

She turned and at that moment Christina screamed. It was loud enough to pierce the ear drums, and it was cut short abruptly with a sound that made Noel freeze and stand rooted to the spot. Christina had done it after all. It had been no bluff.

She forced herself to move, to press her stiffened limbs into action, and she went through the door.

Christina was sprawled across the floor, her skull split open as if it had been an eggshell.

Noel fought the nausea rising from her stomach and went towards her. She had to be dead. She lifted her gently and wished she hadn't. Her face was no longer recognisable and it was covered in blood. She was dead all right.

Noel took her fingers away from her wrist and stood up and a faint sigh echoed behind her. It went on, lasting a few seconds and then the house was as silent as the grave again. Noel felt colder than she'd ever been in her life. The back of her neck prickled as if someone had laid an icy hand on it. What had it been?

She moved sideways towards the library, her heart leaping to her throat as a shadow stepped into the shaft of sunlight streaming in from the open front door.

Against the light and with her dark glasses on he was simply a figure of menace. She bolted into the library as he took a step over the threshold but at the sound of her name she turned and, giving a half sob, ran for him. "Jonas! Oh, Jonas!"

"What's happened?" His arms went around her as she buried her face in his chest. Her body was shaking, tears streaming helplessly down her face.

"She's dead. Oh she's dead Jonas and I did it."

"Don't be silly. Come on now." He put his

hands on her shoulders and pushed her back, whipping out his handkerchief and pulling the dark glasses off her face to wipe the tears away.

He gave an exclamation as he saw her eye. "How did you do that?"

"It was John. Something she said to him." She glanced at the body and started crying again.

"Hush now. Have you phoned for a doctor? For the police?"

"No. It only just happened."

"Come on, sit down." He pushed her into a chair and pushed his handkerchief into her hand. "Wipe your face and blow your nose and let's have no more tears. I'll get you a drink."

His prosaical air calmed her better than any soothing words. She blew her nose hard and meekly took the brandy he bestowed on her.

As she sipped it she heard him on the phone. First to Dr. Shepherd and then to the police. An accident he called it.

"Right," he said, returning. "Now tell me what you are doing here."

"She asked me to come. And—and when I got here she was up there. She said if I didn't promise to go away and never see you again she'd kill herself like Lydia did and I'd be blamed for it."

"And you took no notice?"

"No. I couldn't believe she'd throw her life away—and then I got frightened. I did promise. I *did*. But when I got outside I heard her scream and . . ." She swallowed hard, gripping the brandy glass tightly. "And there she was."

"Did anyone see you here?"

"No. She said Lady Valerie was out for the day and she'd given the servants the afternoon off."

"Go on back to the farm then. Quickly. Deny you've ever been here."

A car engine sounded, sweeping up outside. "Go on," he said. "The back way. Run."

She ran, still holding the brandy glass, not realising it was still in her hand until she had to struggle to open the door. There was a door handle and a yale lock on it. She put the glass down on the kitchen table. The car had been Dr. Shepherd's. She heard his voice as she cautiously opened the door and pulled it behind her and then she ran as fast as she could until a crippling stitch in her side reduced her to a stumbling walk.

It seemed an eternity before the farm came

into sight, nestling in its hollow, promising safety and security.

She stopped to get her breath. The cows were on their way along the road, the cowman chasing a frisky newcomer to the herd who wanted to go the other way.

She cut down across the field and took the stepping stones across the brook, ducking under the willows. There was blood on her sleeve and spots of it on her trousers where she had knelt down. If she went in the back way Mrs. Cassell would be sure to notice. But the french windows were locked. She stepped back. There was another way. The elm outside her bedroom window. She'd used it before. But then she'd been a child and it had been an adventure. She regarded the dimensions dubiously. Jumping from the window ledge to swing hand over hand from the branch above her window seemed not only foolish now but downright impossible. But if she wanted to avoid anyone seeing the blood on her clothes she had to do it.

She put her foot in the first fork and hauled herself up. There was no doubt about it. Climbing trees was purely an art to be exercised by small wiry bodies. She flinched as a twig dug into her cheek and others caught at her clothing. The bark was rough and her hands felt raw. Her feet had lost their skill. She squirmed up through a narrow space and came out on the branch which led to her window. It had diminished over the years. She was . . . how much heavier? She made a painful calculation. It wasn't necessary to be an engineer to work out that the slender branch which had borne her weight years ago might now give way under the strain. Had she really swung on it?

She sat down on it, edging herself along inch by inch, her heart leaping to her throat as it started to bend ominously. It was level with the window-ledge and she was too far to jump.

Her eyes were drawn to the ground and instead of the sprouting grass she saw a chessboard of black and white marble. She closed her eyes, the sickness rising to her stomach again. She was going to fall, exactly as Christina had done, and her body would lie crumpled on the ground.

"Hold on," Sharon cried urgently. "Don't move."

Noel's eyes flew open. Sharon was at the window. She disappeared at once and so fleeting was Noel's glimpse that she wondered if she could have imagined it but within seconds

Sharon had reappeared with a pair of step-ladders. She thrust them out over the window ledge to rest the other end on the branch beyond Noel. "Come on," she said encouragingly.

Noel transferred her weight onto the ladder; first her hands and then a knee. The ladder dipped and Sharon vanished. Noel gripped on so tightly it would have taken a chisel to straighten her fingers. Grimly she started to crawl along. The sweat was running into her eyes by the time she reached the window ledge.

Sharon had flung one arm through the ladders and was hanging on to the chest of drawers, her feet wrapped around the legs of it.

As Noel tumbled into the room she released her grip, breathing hard. "I thought I was going to take off there for a moment. What took you so long?"

"A man with a scythe had a hold on my ankles."

"I believe you." She extricated herself with some difficulty and got to her feet, rubbing her arm. "You'll oblige me by not precipitating a heart attack ever again. Whose blood is that? Hers?"

"Yes."

"She's dead then." It wasn't a question. Noel confirmed it flatly.

There was a brief silence and then Sharon said briskly, "You'd better give me those clothes. I'll get rid of them for you."

"I didn't kill her, Sharon."

"It was an accident? I told you not to go. I warned you. What happened? Did you fight?"

"I never touched her. She killed herself."

Sheer disbelief crossed Sharon's face. "Not that one," she said positively. "You'll never get anyone to believe that."

"That's what *she* said," Noel said tonelessly and began to pull off her jumper.

"I'll put these ladders back," Sharon said. "I take it no one saw you?"

"No."

"It's just as well." She manipulated the ladders easily and left on the dark words, returning to bundle up Noel's clothes. "You'd better wash your face," she said, regarding Noel's face critically. "You're bleeding."

"Leave those. I'll hide them."

"Where?" Sharon said bluntly. "They'd be found. They'll be on to you right away. You know it. That's why you ran. Or are you afraid of trusting me? I could land you in it right now without this bundle."

"Why don't you?"

"Let's say I was brought up the hard way. The police are my natural enemies. Besides, I never did like that bitch. She acted as if she owned us body and soul and was even worse than your sister-in-law to work for."

"I didn't know you worked at the manor," Noel said in surprise.

"And why should anyone tell you? The likes of us are anonymous bodies." There was a bitter twist to Sharon's mouth. "We have feelings—the same as you people. And we can love and hate in equal measure." She put the bundle under her apron and turned towards the door, pausing for one last shot. "Mrs. Fenton sacked me for stealing a ring. She would have had me up in court if her husband hadn't stopped her. I'd help anyone who got into trouble over her so you needn't worry that I'll come by later with a bill for this. Blackmail isn't my line either."

The door was closed quietly and Noel stared at it. There was a wealth of bitterness stored behind Sharon's pretty face. She had only let the tip show.

But she couldn't worry about that now. She had to think, to act.

She went along to the bathroom and scrubbed her skin until it felt raw. She felt dirty and unclean. She had been the cause of another person's death. Nothing she could say would excuse the fact. What was Jonas doing now? Did he think like Sharon? That Christina would never have killed herself?

She washed her hair and examined her face. The scratch could have been caused by a hand raking at her face. There were other little scratches that ran parallel to it. She piled the makeup on and went back to her room. She was waiting. She didn't know what for but something was going to happen. She could feel it in her bones.

They came just after six o'clock. She heard the car and then the ring on the doorbell. Sharon answered it and then Noel heard Nicola. "Miss Noel Clare? No, I'm sorry. She's not in at the moment. She went over to the manor for lunch and hasn't yet returned."

"No, Nicola. I didn't go." Noel stood at the top of the stairs. She was surprised how steady her voice was.

There were two of them. They stood in the

hall, alert and expectant, not at all like her idea of plainclothes men, big and stolid in heavy overcoats and trilby hats. One of them was wearing a sheepskin jacket, the bulk misleading. He was tall and thin with a narrow, clever face and watchful eyes. The other stood a little behind him. He looked a city man, discreetly dressed, fitting in anonymously among all the crowds thronging the tubes at rush hours.

"Then where have you been all afternoon?" Nicola exclaimed in surprise. Noel could have throttled her. "Hiding away in your room?" Her voice altered as Noel came down the stairs. "You've not been quarrelling with John again, have you?" she said sharply.

"I've not seen John."

"But your face . . ." She caught herself up. "I'm sorry. We don't want to display our family squabbles, do we? These two men want to see you, Noel. They're from the police."

"Yes?" She stood at the bottom of the stairs, her hand poised on the balustrade. Keep calm she told herself, waiting politely as they introduced themselves.

The one in the sheepskin jacket was Detective Inspector Powell, the one behind, Detective

Sergeant Watkins. They had come from Elmsbury to investigate the murder of Christine Fenton.

"And you've come to see me?" She managed to inject surprise in her voice. "How can I help you?"

"We understand you were invited to lunch with Mrs. Fenton. Are you claiming now that you didn't go?"

She didn't like the sound of that. Claiming! It was Powell who was doing the talking. He watched her like a cat at a mousehole, ready to pounce at the first mistake.

"I had lunch here," she said. "In the kitchen with Mrs. Cassell and Sharon."

"And afterwards?"

"I went to my room, read for a little while, dozed off and then had a bath and washed my hair."

"Can anyone vouch for that?"

"Why should they?"

"Mrs. Fenton left a letter behind. She told of your affair with her husband. She said she was afraid you were going to kill her because she wouldn't agree to a divorce. The letter was unfinished. She heard you calling her."

"In the first place I am not having an affair

with her husband. In the second, whether she agrees to a divorce or not is . . . was wholly immaterial. If Jonas Fenton wanted a divorce all he had to do was wait. Surely you know that, Inspector? I don't have to explain the laws on divorce to you?"

"But supposing you didn't want to wait? Supposing you were afraid you might lose him?"

"Supposing I bring down my passport? Supposing you do some adding up? I've been in America for nearly seven years and I only got back three days ago."

"We know that."

"Then why are you here? All this could have nothing to do with me."

"Perhaps you'd like to read the letter."

Noel took it reluctantly. She didn't want to read it at all.

There was no salutation. It stated bluntly: "I am afraid." She blinked, forcing herself to concentrate. She wanted to sit down but she too was afraid. Afraid the police would take it as a sign of weakness.

"Noel wants to see me dead," were the next words.

She moved to a chair. Weakness or not she had to sit down at that.

"Last night she admitted it in front of all my friends. She wants to marry Jonas, to live here at the manor and enjoy all the money. And to do that I'll have to die. Divorce, she said, but she knows that won't give her what she wants. She's greedy. She wants everything. They were together on Wednesday night and Jonas didn't return until morning. They weren't even discreet about it. They are trying to bring shame on me so that I will kill myself as Lydia did—or perhaps they are trying to make it appear that I have a good motive for killing myself for when they murder me. I read death in her eyes last night. She would like to murder me. If Jonas has to wait for a divorce I think he'll discover her true colours. I've asked her to lunch today to offer her some money. She might settle for a lump sum instead of an uncertain future for I'll tell her I mean to fight. Jonas is infatuated. I know all the signs. I've seen it before. But this time it's more serious. Since he came back from America there has been a change in him. They must have met out there and planned what they were going to do to me. She knew all about Adele. She is playing her game. And she'll make him help her. God help me, for there is no one I can turn to. Jonas is due back from London any time now. I have to show him what she is really like or I am lost. Believe me, though, if murder is what they plan, look closely at my death. Never believe I would kill myself—I could not. Ever!

"I hear her calling my name now. She is late and I can't help wondering why. Has she waited for Jonas? I will go down to meet her and pray that I will return to destroy this letter."

"She didn't return of course," Powell said as Noel raised her eyes. "Do you still claim you didn't see her?"

"You prefer to believe the ravings of what was obviously a very sick woman? She killed herself. I had nothing to do with it."

"And you weren't having an affair with Jonas Fenton?"

"I was not."

"You didn't stay overnight with him at 'The Ship' in Elmsbury?"

"I stayed alone," Noel said coldly.

"You didn't meet in America?"

"No."

"Are you in love with him? Do you want to marry him?"

"I think we'd better get a solicitor in before you answer any more questions," Nicola interrupted swiftly as Noel hesitated at that.

"I believe we've found out all we want to know for the moment," Powell remarked with bland smoothness. "You *will* be staying here for the next few days, won't you?"

Noel nodded dumbly and he took the letter from her nerveless fingers. Her thumb print stood out, a globule of sweat staining the shiny paper of the photostated copy of the letter. She suddenly remembered the brandy glass she'd left on the kitchen table and from the look on the inspector's face he'd read the thought. His lips curved slightly. "We'll be in touch," he said.

Noel moved into the sitting room as Nicola showed them out. She felt limp and exhausted. They'd find out she was at the manor. They were bound to. And if they took any notice of that letter . . .

"They can't seriously suspect you of murder," Nicola said cheerfully as Noel sank into a chair. "They'd have whipped you off to the police station if they did."

"Christina must be—must have been mad," Noel said, leaning back and closing her eyes.

"What did the letter say?"

"That she was afraid I was going to murder her. Me and/or Jonas. She was a little muzzy on that. In one line we were in collusion, the next she was going to show Jonas what a tramp I was."

"You need a drink," Nicola said in bracing accents.

"No. No, thanks."

"Poor Christina." Nichola poured herself one. "What a way to go. I wonder if she had a premonition last night."

"She had a premonition all right. She knew exactly what she was going to do."

"Get herself murdered?" Nicola turned round, her brows raised.

"She killed herself. I tell you I know she did."

"Not her," Nicola said emphatically. "Never in a thousand years. No, it was probably Jonas. It usually is the husband in cases like this and heaven knows she was no wife for a man like him."

"Jonas?" Noel snapped, roused completely at that. "Ridiculous!"

"You don't know him or anything about his life," Nicola said in amusement. "How could you? You said yourself you were only a child when you went away. And you've had . . . how long with him since your return?"

Noel opened her mouth to argue and then saw the futility of it. There was no way of telling Nicola that the time they had spent together couldn't be measured in the ordinary way. Nicola was too much a woman of the world. She would laugh. And maybe she'd be right in doing so. But Jonas wasn't a murderer. She would have staked her life on that.

The evening dragged by. They had dinner—John, Nicola and Rosemary and herself. It was a grim silent meal.

John didn't speak once. Rosemary excused herself as soon as it was over but when Noel attempted to follow her example Nicola said, "Don't go. I want to talk. I can't stand all this gloom."

"A friend of ours has been murdered," John said heavily with a lowering glance at Noel.

"Well, Noel didn't do it," Nicola declared impatiently "And besides Christina wasn't a close friend—not of yours anyway, so don't pull the hypocrite act on me."

"She was close enough to know just what to

say to set him off last night," Noel said coldly. "She even boasted she could do it again."

"Really?" Nicola said with interest. "What did she say to you, John?"

"It's none of your business."

"Is that so? You'd want to know what it was all about if Jonas whispered in *my* ear."

"Just let me catch him." John got up as Sharon came in to clear the table and he helped her stack things on the trolley.

She smiled her thanks and wheeled it out with a sidelong glance at Noel. Everything okay? it asked. Noel gave a slight nod but it was an unpleasant reminder that everything was not okay, far from it.

"Don't think you're going to get out of answering," Nicola said as he closed the door behind Sharon and switched on the television set. "I want to know what she said."

John turned round dourly but before he could say anything the doorbell rang.

It was a loud, insistent ring and it went again before Sharon had time to answer it.

Nicola stiffened, Noel froze, even John was motionless as they waited for Sharon to announce who it was. Before she could do that, however, Noel had recognised the slow drawl of the man who had entered. She felt the warmth return to her limbs but then the dismay came. What was Doug doing here? She didn't want him around. Not here. He would be in the way.

She ran to the door and pulled it open. "Doug!"

"Noel, my honey. What's wrong? I came as soon as I could." He came close, holding her by the shoulders to regard her searchingly. "You look terrible. What's happened to your face?"

She brushed that aside. "An accident. What do you mean? You came as soon as you could?"

"You sent for me, didn't you?" He saw the answer on her face and his mouth went up resignedly. "I might have known it. You wouldn't say you needed me if the Indians had you tied to the stake and I was the only white man around for a hundred miles. Someone thinks you need me though. Here's the cable. 'Come at once. I need you. Noel.'"

She regarded it incuriously. Easy enough to trace it. There was no doubt it would have been sent from the farm by phone. The address from her missing envelope, the same three suspects

—John, Nicola and Rosemary. It was a waste of time thinking about it.

"Who's your friend?" Nicola cooed sweetly behind her.

Reminded of her manners, Noel made the introductions, amused to see that even John made an effort to be affable. Nicola of course was all over Doug. It wasn't every day she received such a man in her house. He sat in the most comfortable chair in the room exuding his own particular brand of charm, quietly courteous, answering Nicola's questions with patience and humour. He'd had a meal but Nicola insisted on having toasted sandwiches and coffee prepared for him. Then she insisted he stayed at the farm and wouldn't hear of him going off to find a hotel. She told him he'd come in time for the party, he had to stay for that, and she bore him off to show him his room, more animated than Noel had ever seen her.

"She was like that when I first met her," John said, his efforts at civility making him forget his hostility towards his sister. His tone didn't make it seem a wholly pleasant memory. "Doug seems a nice character."

"He is, exceptionally so."

"And you make a fool of yourself over Fenton." John shook his head but it was more with weariness than any forceful emotion. "You'll be sorry. You don't know how much." He got up. His shoulders sagged and his head was bowed. He looked a lot older than his years. "I'm going to bed. Goodnight."

"Goodnight." Noel had difficulty in saying it normally. There was an overwhelming pity in her for John. Had there ever been a time when he had been happy? Could he remember how it had been when their father was alive and he had hoped for something more when he married Nicola.

She picked up one of the sandwiches Doug had left and bit into it absently, glancing up as Nicola came in and headed straight for the fireplace, piling the logs on as if set for a long evening. "Doug is unpacking," she said. "He'll be down in a minute. He's an attractive man, isn't he? That tan . . . and that white blond hair. There'll be a stampede towards him tomorrow. I'll have to—" She broke off abruptly. "What's that little smile for?"

"Sorry, I wasn't aware I was smiling," Noel said, startled at the accusing glare in Nicola's eyes.

"No? You're so smug, Noel! You can't imagine for a moment that anyone else has a chance when you're around. Do you think he'll still stand by when he learns you came back to break up a marriage?"

"That's not true," Noel said quietly.

"No. And of course you didn't murder Christina." She straightened up, the poker in her hand. "You didn't go to see her this afternoon either. You looked those policemen right in the eyes and lied without a tremor. I believed you—anyone would have believed you—but a liar has to have a good memory. You've seen Christina today, you talked with her. By your own words, you admitted it. Do you remember saying Christina was close enough to know how to set John off? She even boasted she could do it again, you said. Now what do you imagine the police would think of that?"

6

THEY wouldn't be at all surprised. Not if they had already found the brandy glass and compared the prints.

Noel regarded Nicola's triumphant expression curiously, watching it fade and uncertainty take its place. What did she expect to see? Fear? Desperation? Was she waiting for a plea for silence, anticipating the delight of having her at her mercy?

"Doesn't it worry you?" she said at last.

"Should it?"

"You think I won't tell them? But John might start to wonder. He'd tell them. He'd think it his duty."

"I'm scared to death."

Nicola replaced the poker and crossed slowly to the cabinet. She poured herself a large brandy. "I don't understand you," she said blankly. "What makes you tick? What goes on behind that poker face? In your position I'd be terrified."

"I didn't murder her. I've no reason to be terrified."

"Then why didn't you tell the truth?" she said at once.

Noel shrugged her shoulders. "In the circumstances it seemed the wiser course of action."

"No! You were frightened. You panicked." Nicola laughed suddenly. "Don't worry. I won't say anything. As a matter of fact I'm too relieved to find that you're human after all."

She sat down gracefully, crossing her legs at the ankles. "You *are* frightened now, aren't you?"

Doug saved her from admitting it. "Noel? Frightened?" he said, smiling at her from the doorway. "She doesn't know the meaning of the word."

"I don't think she's quite as you'd like to think," Nicola said with a laugh and she took a deep swallow from her brandy glass.

Noel waited for it but Nicola made no mention of Jonas or Christina. "We all try to hide our fears," she said. "It's up to you men to find out what they are and help to get rid of them. Now what can I get you to drink, Doug? Sit down and make yourself at home."

"You'll excuse me, won't you? I think I'll go to bed," Noel said, rising to her feet. "I'm very tired."

"I'm not surprised," Nicola said, but Doug rose too. "Don't rush away. We've things to talk about."

"Not now . . . tomorrow. Goodnight, Doug. Nicola will explain things to you."

Let her say what she would. Doug would find out one way or the other. She went up to her room and lay on the bed. It was after midnight before they came up. She gave them half an hour to settle down and then quietly rose and stole down the stairs.

The moon was high and the grass frosty. It crackled beneath her feet and the snap of a twig sounded like a pistol shot. She glanced over her shoulder as she crossed the brook. The farmhouse was in darkness and yet she felt unseen eyes watching her. She walked swiftly, not allowing herself to be nervous. This was her country. No one was lurking in the shadows. She had nothing to be afraid of. She could run, she could outpace anyone or anything. She stopped, listening hard.

An owl hooted, there was a scurry in the underbrush, a fox barked close at hand. Natural sounds. Not made by man.

A cloud blanked out the moon, the trees became a dark solid mass. She hesitated, glancing back towards the farmhouse. She was out of her mind. What did she hope to achieve by going to the manor? Jonas would be asleep. The doors would be barred, the windows securely latched, the servants would be there. They might be roused and then there would be more talk. There was no doubt what they would think and say. Better to wait until daylight, better still to wait until they could meet in a natural way. And when would that be? Would he go out riding in the morning or were the police watching him?

The husband . . . usually the husband. She had heard Dr. Shepherd's car. Why hadn't she heard Jonas drive up? And that long sigh that had echoed through the house. She knew what it was now. It had taken only a casual question at dinner to find out that there was a lift at the manor. A fact that should have been obvious. Christina couldn't wheel her chair up and down the stairs.

Someone else had been in the house. Someone had used the lift as she stood staring down at Christina. And then Jonas had walked in.

She closed her eyes. She had to see him. She had to. She needed the reassurance he could give her. If her faith in him faltered, her faith in life itself was lost.

She turned her back on the farmhouse and headed resolutely towards the wood. She should have brought a torch. There would have been one around somewhere if she had only looked for it. The darkness was a tangible thing under the trees, closing around her like a blanket. She looked up at the sky. The black mass of cloud moving across the moon was almost by. It thinned and then was gone and the moonlight filtered through the bare gaunt branches and fell on the ground. She had strayed away from the path. A fallen tree trunk blocked her way. She worked round it. The path didn't matter. She was going in the right direction.

Another cloud came up and she stopped again. Close by a twig snapped. She backed towards the trunk of a huge elm. A light bobbed in the darkness to her left. She waited and let it go by. A poacher? Or Jonas? Or someone else?

She turned and followed that bobbing light. She'd see when the moon came clear.

The cloud was thinning again. She glanced up at the sky and her foot went down into a rabbit hole. She cried out involuntarily as she hit the ground. Her ankle felt as if it were broken. She rolled over, her face taut with the pain. The light ahead had vanished. She wasn't surprised. She waited, her ears straining for the faintest sound.

He was coming back. No city man. His feet tested and then moved on, cautiously and with knowledge. It was Jonas. She knew it as certainly as if he had shouted her name and the fear left her. "I'm here," she cried out in a low voice.

The beam shone out, spun around and then caught her full in the face. She blinked and he killed the beam. "I thought it was you," he said, and there wasn't any surprise in his voice either. "Were you going to the manor?"

"Yes. Were you going to the farm?"

"Yes." He laughed softly. "Aren't we a pair? I had no idea what I'd do when I got there. Are you all right?"

"Of course."

"Did the police come?"

"Yes."

"She left a letter."

"Yes. They showed it to me."

There was a silence but it wasn't a bad one. Everything was going to be all right. She had been silly to worry. "They'll find out I was there," she said.

"I'm afraid so." He sighed. "I wanted to keep you out of it. If I'd had more time . . ."

He squatted down beside her. "Did you hurt yourself?"

"It's all right now."

His hands were gentle but she winced as he examined her ankle. "Maybe a sprain," he said, "but nothing serious. You're an idiot. You know that, don't you? Coming out like this."

"Then what are you?"

"I'm in love with you. In such a state a man can be excused all kinds of idiocy."

"Jonas . . . The police said it was murder. Are they going by that letter alone?"

"I don't know."

"Why did you make me run away?"

"It seemed a good idea," he said reluctantly.

"Do you think I killed her?"

"Don't be silly." He stood up abruptly. "Can you walk?"

"Jonas . . . You don't believe she killed herself either, do you?"

"Come on. I'll take you back."

"Jonas, you have to answer me. What do you think happened there?"

"I don't know. An accident maybe. However it happened you mustn't blame yourself." He took a deep breath. "You don't imagine it was the first time she got her own way by threatening to kill herself, do you? It was how she kept me to heel. All these years—" His voice was harsh. "That accident in the car. I couldn't believe she'd done it deliberately but there was always that doubt. She had me over a barrel and she knew it. Do you know what it's been like? No, of course you don't. You can have no conception of it. My brave, beautiful wife presenting a valiant face to the world. Breaking her back was the best thing that ever happened to her. She revelled in the power it gave her, she basked in the admiration everyone showed her. She could do what she liked and say what she liked and she had a hold on me that she thought I would never have the courage to break. What man *could* break away under the threat of causing someone's death?"

"But you were going to do it."

"Oh yes," he said softly. "I thought I'd lost you and then there you were. I couldn't let you go again."

He pulled her to her feet and held her, his face sombre in the moonlight, and then suddenly he swung her off her feet cradling her in his arms.

She protested, but not very hard. Her ankle was beginning to throb.

"You might wrench it again," he said, "and do some real damage." He carried her easily and in silence and she lay there, content for the moment, safe in the circle of his arms, certain and sure that whatever lay ahead they had the strength between them to weather it. He set her down by the brook. "The next few days are going to be hard," he said. "But we'll come through. Trust in me."

"I always will."

"You can get back in?"

"I left the door on the latch."

"Goodnight then." He didn't kiss her.

She hesitated and then walked away, limping a little. Before she turned the corner of the house she looked back. He was still standing by the brook. She stopped, raising her hand but he made no movement. He mustn't be able to see her she decided; not against the dark background of the house. But why hadn't he kissed her? With his wife dead that day! Had she no understanding?

She hadn't told him about the lift. She hadn't

found out why she hadn't heard his car. Trust him. She did, she did. But what kind of fear was it that stilled her tongue?

Her dreams that night were haunted by Christina. Christina dead, Christina alive, Christina as a pale vengeful ghost shrieking that she'd never let him go.

She was glad when dawn broke and she could get up although she had barely had more than a couple of hours sleep all told.

Tempest was glad to see her and she rode him fiercely to get the dreams out of her mind. Along the ridge, down across the river and up to the tower. But this time there was no dark rider at their heels. She let the reins fall, sitting very still in the saddle. A heavy mist hung over the low ground, damp and ghostly. Nothing moved. It was as though the whole world held its breath, waiting . . .

Jonas wouldn't come of course. Too many eyes, too many ears. There would be too much talk as it was.

She turned Tempest homewards, tired now, drooping in the saddle. What was to come?

A police car waited at the farm to take her into Elmsbury.

She didn't falter. John was in the yard, his

147

face a mask. She slid out of the saddle and he nodded to one of the men to take Tempest away.

"I tried to get hold of a solicitor," Nicola said in a low voice. She was wringing her hands, a frightened look in her face. "But, Saturday morning . . . The office is closed and no one is answering the phone at his home." She took a step forward, lowering her voice to a bare whisper. "I didn't tell them anything. I swear I didn't."

"I suppose I know who to thank," Noel said wearily, glancing at John. He stood like a rock, gaunt and unmoving with folded arms; without compassion, without love. A man she could still pity.

"They're waiting for you," he said.

"They've not got a warrant," Nicola said breathlessly. "You could refuse to go."

Noel smiled without humour. "I don't think that would get me very far." She glanced at the car. A uniformed man was at the wheel, another waited stolidly. "Doug?"

"He's still sleeping. I didn't like to wake him. What shall I say to him?"

Noel smiled faintly. "Maybe I won't be long. Keep him entertained."

She walked towards the car and got in. The door was closed on her smartly, the second policeman getting in at the front besides the driver. The car turned and she glanced back, her gaze going beyond Nicola and John to the farmhouse. Rosemary was at the window of her room. As her eyes met Noel's she drew back. Her face was blank, devoid of expression, but there was satisfaction in the way she closed the window. It was as if she said, good riddance.

Noel turned her eyes ahead. The two men in front were silent. The radio crackled, a voice giving instructions, going on and on, a monotonous droning that soon made the words merge and become merely sound. She was glad when they reached the town.

The police station was a new building, a pleasing rectangular design in red brick but inside it was cold and bare and there was a smell that stuck in her nostrils; disinfectant, carbolic, and a rank, unclean odour that made her think of decay, not of the flesh but of the mind. The close association of the law against the unlawful; ordinary men in constant touch with evil, hardened and coarsened by it, callous to the feelings of the uninitiated.

She was shown into a little room that held a

table and two chairs on either side of it. They left her waiting a long time. She sat unmoving on one of the chairs. Was this the first softening up procedure? She wanted to pace the floor, to open the door and demand to know why they had brought her here. The cold seemed to penetrate through to her bones and then her mind. She'd not eaten, she'd not even had coffee. She glanced at her watch and then checked the desire to look again a few minutes later. If they were watching her from some hidden peephole she wasn't going to give them the smallest satisfaction.

They came for her before she started chewing her nails and she followed a uniformed constable up some stairs and into a bright, airy room. The first person she saw was Jonas and dismay struck her like a blow as he glanced at her and then quickly looked away again. The flesh on his face seemed to have shrunk or been eaten away. The bones were accentuated, his eyes deep pits of despair.

Her gaze went to Powell. He was behind a big desk, leaning back in a swivel chair. His expression was almost one of complacency. She hated him then and maybe she showed it for he smiled and said pleasantly, "Sit down, Miss Clare."

She sat down again; another hard chair. But it was warmer in this room. There was a carpet on the floor. Watkins was over by the window, his eyes on her profile. A uniformed man was seated at the side, a pad on his knee, a pencil poised expectantly.

"Now, Miss Clare," Powell said, still pleasantly, the slight hardening of his voice almost imperceptible. "Tell me again what you did yesterday afternoon."

"I went to the manor," Noel said tiredly. "I was there, I talked to Christina. She was waiting for me in the long gallery. She told me that unless I promised to go away and leave Jonas alone she would kill herself and I would be blamed for it. I didn't believe her but in the end I promised. I was outside the house when I heard her scream. I don't know why she did it. Maybe she didn't believe me."

"Why didn't you tell us this yesterday?"

"It was a shock. I wasn't thinking very straight."

"And now you are?"

"I realise there's no point in lying to you."

She glanced at Jonas, silent, withdrawn, staring straight ahead of him.

"Because you knew we were bound to find out the truth?"

"If you like."

"Who was Lydia?"

He must know. Why ask that? Noel said shortly, "She was the wife of James Fenton and she lived at the beginning of this century."

"And Adele Beaton?"

"His second wife." She wasn't going into any detail.

"She was more than that, as you must know. Did you see in her story a way of getting rid of Christina Fenton?"

"I am not interested in tales of the past. There can be no comparison."

"But you read about her, frequently."

Noel stared and then said bluntly, "What are you getting at?"

"This is yours, is it not?" He pushed a slim pamphlet towards her and her hands went out to lift it, stopping short as she read the title. *A History of Henton*, by the Reverend Horace Mitchell. "Oh, no," she said violently. "You're not getting my fingerprints on that. I've never seen it before in my life."

"But it was in your suitcase and you have evidently studied the tale of Adele. You see . . ." He held it up and the pages parted naturally.

Noel stared at the reproduction of the portrait of Adele at one side; the vitality still blazed through, arrogant and unassailable. The Reverend Horace Mitchell had gone to town on her. "From the first moment she laid her eyes on James Fenton Adele was determined to have him." She skidded along the lines. The old tale. She knew it well. But so did everyone else in Henton. "Some whispered murder but none dared say it aloud. She married her man and bore him a son." Noel tore her eyes away. Her suitcase! Had Christina planted it there? Or someone else?

"It's not mine and I have never seen it before," she said firmly. "And who gave you permission to go through my belongings?"

Powell ignored that. "I expect you'll recognise this," he said. He opened his hand and showed her a gold locket, oval in shape. He touched the catch and opened it. Side by side the two faces stared up at her, Jonas and herself.

She felt the room closing in on her. The

locket was hers, a present from her mother long ago, but the photographs . . . she had never had a photograph of Jonas. "That locket was empty," she said unsteadily. "And I've not worn it for years."

"You weren't wearing it yesterday when you pushed Christina Fenton to her death?"

"She killed herself. I wasn't in the house."

"She was pushed. She fought for her life." His gaze rested reflectively on the scratches on her cheek. "The locket was pulled apart."

"Then if it was pulled with some force I'd have marks around my neck. Would you like to check?"

"You were wearing a heavy knit sweater of fawn wool with a high neck." He picked up a strand of wool and held it up between his fingers. "This was caught in the chain."

"It's not from my sweater," Noel said, but her head was spinning. What had Sharon done with her clothes? All those snags on it. Would the wool match? But it couldn't. It wasn't possible.

"Was it a sudden temptation?" Powell said in a soft voice. "Did you suddenly see a way by which you could get all you wanted? Or did you plan it? Were you helped by Jonas Fenton, the man you loved and wanted for yourself?"

"He wasn't there," Noel said quickly. "She was dead before he came."

"You were there when he arrived?"

"Yes. I heard his car and I ran out to him. He couldn't have had anything to do with it."

Jonas glanced up sharply. She couldn't meet his eyes.

"Now that's very interesting," Powell said musingly. "Mr. Fenton got a taxi from Henton and he paid him off at the gates. You heard his car you said?"

"It must have been the taxi then."

"Let me see." He turned to Watkins. "What would you say the distance was from the gates to the manor house?"

"A mile at least," Watkins said stolidly.

"It was a very quiet afternoon. Sound carries," she said desperately.

"And you ran out to him—and he was there; he'd covered a mile in seconds?"

"I waited."

"Ah, you were expecting him?"

She closed her eyes briefly. This was what came of lying. "He wasn't there," she repeated. "He had nothing to do with it. But there was

155

someone there. As I—as I was standing over Christina I heard the lift go. I didn't know what it was then. It sounded like a long sigh and it frightened me. Later on I realised what it must have been."

"So someone else was in the house now? You see the futility of claiming Mrs. Fenton killed herself? And who was this someone? Who else had a motive for killing her? A stray tramp I suppose? Or a burglar perhaps? Interrupted by Mrs. Fenton?"

"I heard the lift," Noel said shakily. "It's the truth."

"You love this man?" He indicated Jonas abruptly.

"No, she doesn't," Jonas said harshly before she could answer. "How could she? She hardly knows me."

"You met within a day of your arrival. That smacks to me of pre-arrangement. You kept in touch while she was in America, didn't you?"

"No."

"Really?" Powell picked up a piece of paper. "You were in America earlier this year. You went to Florida for a month and stayed at the Milo Hotel. Miss Clare was also in Florida at that time. You didn't meet then?"

"No."

An icy snowball started to form in the pit of Noel's stomach.

"I understand it was on your account that Miss Clare left home," Powell said, his soft voice hardening. "When her brother refused to tell you her whereabouts you employed a detective agency to trace her. During the whole of this seven years you have kept a constant check on her whereabouts. When it was reported to you she was getting friendly with another man you went out there. What happened in that month, Mr. Fenton? Couldn't you bear to think of her falling in love with another man? Did you persuade her to come back here?"

"She didn't know I was there," Jonas said in a strangled voice. "I wanted to make sure she was happy. I wanted to know that the man she picked was a good man, able to look after her as—as I could not."

The ice moved up in Noel's body, freezing every ounce of blood. "Jonas," she whispered. "Oh, Jonas."

He didn't look at her. "Let her go," he said harshly. "I killed my wife."

7

"NO, it's not true. You didn't. You couldn't." Noel sprang up and ran to Jonas, shaking him by the shoulders. "Don't say such a thing. Oh, Jonas . . ." The tears were streaming down her face. She didn't hear Powell's quiet words. Jonas gazed at her and on his face was a look that twisted her heart. "Forget me," he said. "You have a good life ahead of you."

"No! No!"

She pulled away as hands were laid on her, but the grip was firm. She was parted from him and led outside, down the stairs and into another waiting room.

A policewoman took charge of her, the words she uttered unheeded and unheard. Jonas couldn't have killed Christina. "He thinks I did it," she cried. "That's why he's doing this. He thinks *I* did it."

The tears dried up. She took a hold on herself. She washed her face and swallowed the scalding tea the policewoman had brought to her.

158

Her statement was brought in. She read it through and signed it and said she wanted to see Powell again.

"He'll send for you when he wants to see you again," the policewoman said.

"I want to see him now."

"I'm afraid it's impossible."

"Then I'll wait." She stared at the police-woman. She was a plump girl, the uniform emphasising her heavy breasts. She didn't look the type to be in the force. Her face was comely and kind. She should have had a brood of children around her and a man to look after her. She said calmly, "You'll wait a long time."

"He had me in there just to make Jonas crack. All those lies, trying to make it look as if I had done it. Doesn't he care how he gets an arrest?"

"He's a good policeman," the woman said briskly. "If your man is innocent he's nothing to fear. The best thing you can do is to go home now. You'll not achieve anything by staying."

"How could he tell Christina had struggled? How could—" She broke off. Dr. Shepherd would tell her. He'd know.

"I'll go home," she said abruptly.

The policewoman looked startled but she said, "I'll arrange for a car to take you."

The car wasn't necessary. Doug was waiting outside.

"Nicola told me," he said soberly. "Is everything all right?"

"Do I look as if everything is all right?" she said bitterly.

"You need some food. Come and eat."

"No. I must see Dr. Shepherd. They say Christina was murdered. She didn't kill herself. She—"

He took hold of her arm firmly. "You sound hysterical. It's not like you. Have a hot cup of coffee at least."

"You don't understand. Jonas is saying he killed Christina. He thinks I did it. He thinks he's protecting me. They found a book in my suitcase, my locket under Christina with our pictures in it, a strand of wool they said came from my sweater."

"You're not making sense. Tell me all about it, quietly and coherently." He steered her into "The Ship" and to a corner table.

Drinks appeared like magic and then food. Noel ate without noticing. She told Doug everything, right from the time she walked in the farmhouse, and was too full of her own troubles to notice the expression fading from his eyes, leaving them cold and hard.

"It's the end of the world to you, isn't it? What if he did do it? It's possible."

"He'd never have let me be incriminated," she cried.

"No, of course not. He's too wonderful for words. Keeping tabs on you all that time! Are you sure you didn't meet in Florida? You'd showed no inclination to want to go home until then."

"And I showed it then? Oh no, Doug. I didn't decide on that until you asked me to marry you and you know when that was. Don't you start thinking like a policeman too. I never hid anything from you and I'm not going to start now. If Christina didn't kill herself and arrange for those things to be found then someone else did. Someone who hates me. That's not Jonas."

"He's quite a womaniser, I hear."

"Women are attracted to him certainly. I have no illusions on that score. Who told you that? Rosemary or Nicola?"

"John, as a matter of fact. He was giving me some advice, telling me to take you away from here. And you know something, Noel, I'm very tempted to take his advice. I can make you forget this bloke. I was a fool to let you come back in the first place."

"You couldn't have stopped me," Noel said gently. "I'm sorry, Doug, but that's how it is. I love him and if I can't have him I'll not marry anyone."

"You really have made up your mind on that? Nothing I can say will make you change your mind?"

"No."

"I don't believe you. Oh, I don't doubt that's how you feel now, but you are in an over-wrought, highly emotional state. I think you'll see reason when you've had time to calm down. He'll be in prison a long time, Noel."

"You've not taken in one word I've said, have you? He didn't do it. He *did not do it!*"

She stood up abruptly. "I want to see Dr. Shepherd now. You can lend me the money and I'll go alone. I came out without my bag."

"You're not going anywhere alone while I'm around," he said grimly. "And where are those dark glasses of yours? People are staring."

"It's a bit late in the day to start worrying about people staring." She paused. She had caught sight of Barry and Marion at the table where they'd been sitting that first time she'd lunched here. How long ago that seemed.

Barry stood up as they approached. He was sober now, very much so. "It's a terrible thing," he said. "We can't believe it."

"She loved life so much," Marion said in a breathless gasping way. "I understand they've arrested Jonas. We thought—well—" She stopped, looking at her husband for help. He gave it without a thought for tact. "We heard they'd hauled you in too."

"We won't say a word about what happened at the dinner party," Marion added earnestly. "You can rely on us."

"What do you mean?" Noel asked blankly.

Marion uttered a nervous little laugh and coughed, covering her mouth with her hand. "Nicola called us this morning. She wanted us to promise that we wouldn't tell the police of the quarrel you had with Christina."

"I wouldn't have called it a quarrel myself," Noel said coldly.

"No, of course not. That's what we'll say." Barry shot a warning glance at his wife. "I'm glad to see they didn't keep you there long. Nicola was almost frantic with worry."

She was fighting a losing battle if she expected everyone to keep quiet about the dinner party. How did she expect John to react to such a request for a start? If he'd told the police she'd been to the manor that afternoon he wouldn't keep silent on what Christina had said to her.

And Lady Valerie and Dr. Shepherd! Noel went hot at the thought of such a request being put to them.

"Don't keep anything back on my account," she said fiercely. "I've got nothing to hide."

Barry looked startled for a moment and then hastened to reassure her. "Of course you haven't. That's what I told Nicola. The minute you start trying to keep something under wraps people begin to wonder why. Poor Nicola! She wasn't thinking straight. She was terrified they were going to charge you."

"Nicola! Terrified?"

"And hasn't she reason to be?" Marion said hotly. "We all heard you. 'Over my dead body,' she said. And you looked at her and it was like a death sentence being pronounced. 'So be it,' you said—and the next day she's dead. What do you expect us to think—that it was an act of God? You're—"

164

Her husband laid a restraining hand on her arm and she finished in a choking gasp. "She doesn't mean anything," he said easily. "She's upset. We all are. We'll see you tonight, Noel."

Noel passed on blindly and Doug took her arm outside. "I could have been anyone," he said angrily. "How could they talk like that!"

"Oh, they knew who you were," Noel said. Her eyes felt hot and heavy. "Nicola wouldn't have lost any time in describing you. I'm sorry I didn't introduce you. They're two of Nicola's friends. They don't know me very well and Marion's probably being bitchy because her husband was too friendly with me the other night."

"Did you say that?"

"So be it? Yes. Foolish of me, wasn't? But I didn't know she was going to be dead the next day."

"Don't worry." He smiled at her. "It will all sort itself out. Where does this Dr. Shepherd live? Nicola lent me her car."

He was holding a surgery. They waited until he had finished and then Noel went in alone.

He bounded to his feet when he saw her. "My dear child. What's happened to you now?

Nicola's been on the phone with some garbled tale about your being arrested."

"They let me go. Jonas said he killed Christina. Dr. Shepherd, you must help him. He couldn't have done it. He only said it to protect me."

"You *were* there then?" Dr. Shepherd sat down abruptly. "I wondered. Your perfume. I noticed it the other night and I could smell it there."

"Did you tell the police that?"

He regarded her searchingly, a fierce glare in his eyes. "My dear child," he said with some asperity, "anyone can buy a bottle of perfume." His gaze softened. "Sit down," he said gently. "You didn't sleep much last night, did you? And what happened to your eye?"

"It was John," she said dully. "Dr. Shepherd, did you find a locket under the body?"

"I didn't touch her," he said. "I saw at once there was nothing I could do."

"They say she was murdered, that she didn't kill herself; she struggled. Would it have been easy to send her over that rail?"

"Her chair was pushed through the balustrades," he said slowly. "It wouldn't have taken much force. Those balustrades were not built to resist any strong pressure."

"But—" she stopped, nonplussed. "I didn't see the chair."

"No. Someone kept tight hold of that."

"I see." She closed her eyes, going back twenty-four hours. The scream, the time she had waited. But whoever had killed Christina hadn't known there would be that time lag. Supposing he—or she—hadn't been able to wear gloves. They'd have had to wipe their fingerprints off the chair before they could run. And how much better to point to murder by holding on to the chair. Christina might have driven herself against the balustrades but the chair would have gone over too. No, she had to face it. There really was no doubt that it was murder. At least nothing she could have said would have prevented that. She should have felt some relief but she felt worse. Jonas had known it was murder then. He had known last night, maybe as soon as he entered the house. Those damned dark glasses. They must have blinded her. She should have seen the broken balustrades. Jonas had seen them. That was why he had made her run. He had suspected she had done it even then. She felt sick. No wonder he hadn't kissed her last night. And after what he'd learned that morning it wasn't surprising that he hadn't been able to meet her eyes.

"I'll take a look at that arm of yours while you're here," the doctor said briskly.

She held it out, not bothering to glance up as the door opened and Dr. Shepherd said, "Wait your turn young man."

"He's with me. Doug Brominsky—Dr. Shepherd."

"You were a long time. I got worried," Doug said.

"You needn't worry about Dr. Shepherd."

"I should think not indeed." Dr. Shepherd gave a bark of laughter. "I'm old enough to be her grandfather."

"Noel didn't mean it in that sense. Did you know someone took a shot at her, doctor? And that someone is trying to frame her for this murder?"

Dr. Shepherd straightened up. "You'd better explain yourself," he said, after a brief appraising stare at Doug.

"What's the matter with her arm?" Doug crossed the floor. "Did your brother do that, too?" he demanded.

"No, this was an accident." She closed her

eyes as the doctor said, "I think we can take those stitches out now. You have good healing flesh, Noel, but I've told you that before, haven't I? A light bandage. We'll let the air get to it." He did his work with deft fingers and then stood up. "Now come and have some tea and do some talking. I can't see anyone hating you so much that they'll do anything to get you out of the way."

Dusk was falling as they left the doctor's house. "He doesn't know what to believe," Doug remarked as he drove carefully along the narrow country lanes, "but one thing is for sure. He's quite certain you didn't do it."

"He's known me for a long time," Noel said. And he had more faith in her than Jonas had. She felt as if she were bleeding from her heart. "Do you think they'll still be questioning Jonas?"

"Could be." He glanced at her swiftly and then returned his attention to the road. "You think it's John, don't you, who wants you out of the way? Why? There's something you've not told me, isn't there?"

"Yes, but it's not important. It had nothing to do with Christina. He wouldn't have killed her to get me out of the way. He hasn't got such a devious mind."

"Who has?"

"I don't know." She was silent for a few minutes and then she said, "Have you met Rosemary yet?"

"There's an unhappy girl," Doug said quietly. "Does she ever smile?"

"Not as if she means it. She claims to hate me too."

"Claims? That's an odd word to use."

She shook her head dubiously. "I don't know if she means it. They say blood is thicker than water but something happened to us when our father died. I think both she and John began to resent me then. My mother favoured me too much. I can see it now and the worst thing about it was that I really didn't care. I was as selfish as they come."

"And have you changed?"

"I suppose you're implying that I haven't. Everyone seems to have a wholly false picture of me in their minds. I'm confident, self assured, afraid of nothing, caring only for my own wants and no one else's. I don't feel a bit like that inside. I'm quaking at the knees right now at the prospect of meeting all those people

Nicola is inviting tonight. I can hear the whispers, see the sidelong glances and I'll know exactly what is on their minds. One way or another they'll decide I'm to blame for Christina's death. That's the way things go. They'll rake up all that gossip of seven years ago and unless I miss my guess they'll have more from Marion. She's exactly the type to spread it around. Nicola must have been out of her mind to phone her with a request to keep quiet. That will be included as an extra piece of spice."

"I'm sure Nicola was only acting for the best."

"I don't doubt it, but honestly! She should know her own friends."

"There's a way of stopping the gossip. I brought this over for you."

He stopped the car and turned towards her, pulling a small box out of his pocket. She stopped him before he opened it. "No. I can't do that, Doug."

"Whoever sent for me had the right idea. You need me."

"As a friend," she cried. "I can't be anything more."

"Very well." His face set grimly. He started the car again.

She sat beside him, feeling miserable and uncertain. Was she making a mistake? He was all that a girl could ask for. But her heart cried out for Jonas. Had they locked him up now? Was he behind bars, caged up like a wild animal? It was wrong. He would die if he were kept there. How long would they give him? A life sentence. Twenty years? But they weren't going to do that to him. Not while she was free to find out who had really killed Christina.

The farmhouse was ablaze with lights. At the sound of the car Nicola came running, wrapping her arms around Noel as she got out of the car. "Marion called. I was so glad, but where have you been? I expected you back hours ago. What happened? She said they'd arrested Jonas."

"They'd not arrested him when I left." Noel disengaged herself. "Would you mind very much if I ducked out of your do tonight?"

"You can't do it," Nicola said matter-of-factly. "Do you want people to think you're afraid of showing your face? Go on up and have a long bath now and put on your most glamorous dress. Doug, put the car in the garage, will you? And then come and have a drink with me while Noel is getting ready."

Noel didn't go straight up to her room but went to see her mother. Rosemary was with her. She looked as if she'd been crying.

"You needn't have upset yourself," Noel said lightly. "As you see, they let me go."

"You flatter yourself. I'd never shed a tear for you."

"For Jonas then? Wouldn't it be a terrible thing if someone had planned the perfect murder with a scapegoat all nicely laid on and the wrong person got arrested for it. Why did you leave that message on the pad, Rosemary? And tell all and sundry about it? Was it just in case something went wrong and you couldn't afford to be the only person who knew I'd be at the manor with Christina?"

"You think I hate you. Is it love you feel for me, that you can accuse me of all these things? My tears weren't for you, nor for Jonas. They were for what might have been. You wouldn't understand that. You don't have any regrets." She closed the book she'd had on her knee. "It's about time the wheel turned and things go my way. You've had your run."

She got up. "I suppose I'd better get ready for the precious party of Nicola's. We must present a united front and show the world we don't believe you're guilty."

Noel stepped in front of her. "Rosemary, where were all my clothes and things put? The old snapshots and bits of jewellery."

"In the attic, I expect. Or are you accusing me of helping myself? You seem to think I'm capable of anything."

"Someone took my locket and cut up a snapshot of me to fit in it, together with one of Jonas."

"Ah . . . I begin to see the light. You've been put in a compromising position. Where was it found—clutched in Christina's dead hand? The silent accusation." She smiled bleakly. "I'm surprised they let you go."

"Jonas said he'd killed his wife."

Rosemary drew her breath in sharply. "He admitted it? He couldn't have been so foolish." She stared at Noel and then said slowly, "It was because of you, wasn't it? All because of you." Her eyes filled with tears. She blinked rapidly but couldn't stop them falling and pushing past Noel she went blindly from the room.

Noel sat down. She couldn't explain her logic even to herself—that in accusing Rosemary she would deny, explain, do something, anything, to prove that the hate she expressed was on the surface only. She didn't want to admit that it went deeper and yet Rosemary seemed determined to let her think otherwise.

Her eyes fell on the pad she had left on her previous visit. Rosemary had been following her example but she couldn't have liked what her mother spelled out. "Help Noel. She needs you."

She looked at her mother. Her eyes were closed, as they had been since she entered the room but her cheek was wet. She leaned closer. The slow tears were forcing themselves out between her closed lids. "Are you awake, Mother?" she asked softly.

The lids lifted fractionally. "You mustn't worry about me," she said. "Everything will turn out all right." Fool that she was. To talk as she did with her mother in the room. "Rosemary wouldn't do anything to hurt me," she went on rapidly. "You know how sisters are. When it comes to the crunch she'll stand by me. Don't fret so." She patted her mother's cheek and made an escape from the room, oppressed by such helpless frustration.

The attic. She'd need the stepladders and a torch. She went down to the kitchen but Mrs.

Cassell and Sharon were frantically busy with the preparations for the party. They stopped long enough to assure themselves she was all right and Sharon told her where the stepladders were and where she might find a torch—in John's office.

She opened the bottom drawer of the desk and found the torch where Sharon thought it might be. John had been doing some work. The Ministry forms littered his desk but on the blotter was a plain sheet of paper. He had been doing some rough balancing. The sheet was almost covered with his laboriously written figures, crossed out and re-written, cut down again and again, but no amount of juggling seemed to produce the figure he wanted.

She moved away quickly as she heard his tread outside. He came in, his face freezing up as he saw her. "What are you doing here?" His eyes went to the desk and he snatched up the sheet of paper.

"I only wanted the torch. Don't worry. I wasn't checking your additions."

"Why did they let you go?"

"I didn't do it, John. Is that a good enough reason for you?"

"You wanted her dead. You said so. And you were there. You lied to the police."

"Did you tell them that?"

"I'll not harbour a murderer in this house. I'll do my duty."

"Why don't you admit it, John? Stop playing the hypocrite! You have your own reasons for getting rid of me but all the juggling in the world won't ease your conscience. Will it help if I tell you I don't want the money? You obviously need it more than I do." She slipped past him and ran up the stairs.

The entrance to the attic was at the end of the passageway; a small trap door set in the ceiling.

She climbed the ladders and pushed it open cautiously, expecting a cloud of dust as it fell. There was dust, but not as much as she expected. The torch picked out an assortment of boxes and some suitcases, an old blanket chest, a rolled up mattress. She lowered the torch and examined the floor. The dust was scuffed but there were no obvious footprints. The general direction showed up however. Grocery cartons; some half dozen of them.

She swung herself up and crawled towards them, a little afraid of putting her foot through the joists. The cartons held her clothes all right, and her books. Could that book on Henton be hers? She might have had a copy. She went through the boxes. There were things she'd forgotten she possessed. Her little bits of jewellery were in a leather box on top of one of the boxes. There were snapshots in a Kodak wallet. She leafed through them. There weren't many. They hadn't been a camera conscious family. She didn't know which one was missing. Whoever had taken it hadn't left the discarded part of it around. She put everything back where it had been. There was nothing to be learned here, only the fact that someone had been up and helped themselves.

She backed out and pulled the trap door down and then went for her bath. Something glamorous. It would have to be the dress she wore for Jonas. Mrs. Cassell had done wonders with it. She had even managed to make a presentable job of the silver slippers.

She piled the makeup on over her eye. Impossible to hide the bruising completely but it was less noticeable and the little minor scratches on her cheek were hidden completely.

The cars had started to arrive. She stayed in her room smoking one cigarette after the other until Doug came for her. "You can't hide for ever," he said. "You look beautiful again. Come down and face them."

The dining room had been cleared of furniture and the carpet rolled back. Some people were dancing. A buffet was spread out on a long table in the hall, the drinks were in the sitting room. The music bounced off the walls and the voices were raised above it. Nicola was darting about from one group to another, happily animated, always with something to say. But she didn't look as if she had a care in the world. And Rosemary too. She was laughing with Dr. Shepherd, with every appearance of enjoying herself. Perceiving Noel, she said something to him and they both moved towards her.

John loomed up. He put a drink in her hand, slapped Doug on the back, his face wreathed in smiles. It would have taken a very acute observer to notice the strain in his eyes.

Then Nicola came, linking her arm affectionately through Noel's. It was more than a united front, it was a blatant display of solidarity.

Throughout the evening one or the other was at her side, steering her through the renewing of old acquaintances and introducing her to new people. Doug was with her almost all the time,

179

attentive and disarmingly charming to all he met.

It was almost possible to see the suspicion fade from people's eyes. Noel felt herself begin to relax. Her strung-up nerves lost their tautness. Sharon was serving champagne and she was attentive in keeping the glasses filled.

"You see, there was nothing to worry about," Doug murmured in her ear as they danced.

"Did you all have a council of war beforehand and decide on your tactics?"

"We discussed the situation certainly."

"And to how many people has Nicola told the glad news?"

"What's that?"

"At least a dozen people have asked me if it's to be a Christmas wedding."

"Well, why not? It's a good time of the year to get married. What did you tell them?"

"I was a coward. I hedged every time." She sighed, resting her head against his chest.

"You'll marry me. There'll be no other course for you to take." His arms tightened confidently around her and she stiffened, pushing herself back from him.

Jonas was in the doorway. Their eyes met and held and there was no one else in the room, no one watching them. They were alone in their own world. And then he glanced at Doug and turned away.

She stood completely still and then broke free from Doug, running for the doorway. "Jonas! Jonas! Wait!"

John blocked her path, Doug caught hold of her, Rosemary and Nicola hurried up, creating their protective barrier once more. "Don't be a fool," Nicola said in a low voice. "What do you think we've been doing all evening?"

"Let me go." She struggled in Doug's arms.

"Don't be foolish, child," Dr. Shepherd added his bit in a stern voice. "This is no place for Jonas tonight. Dance—and smile. You'll do him no good by linking yourself with him."

"But his face—he thought—I have to explain." She pulled herself from Doug's hold and ducked under John's arms, running to the front door.

She was too late. The stop lights of his car glowed in the dark as he braked for the corner and then he had gone with a roar from his engine.

"You *fool*," John said. "You utter fool. Don't you care what people think? Don't you care how much of an exhibition you make of yourself? No one will believe Doug will have you now. You couldn't have made a more public declaration if you'd screamed it from the roof of the town hall."

"Leave her alone, John," Nicola said warningly.

"Leave her alone! To go after him? She'll not see him again—not while I have anything to do with it. Go to your room, Noel."

"Very well." She went with dignity. She had to change anyway. She couldn't go through the woods dressed as she was.

Only when she tried to get out again the door wouldn't budge.

She pulled at the handle fruitlessly. He must have wedged something under the handle at the other side.

She kicked at the door, cursing him wildly and then realising the futility of it, went to sit on the bed. She'd wait then. When everyone had gone she'd climb out of the window. Not by the tree. Sheets.

She hauled them off the bed and knotted them together. They should be long enough. She went to the window, drawing back quickly. John was there with one of the farm men. They were chaining two of the dogs to the base of the tree.

She pulled up the window, furiously angry. "You won't stop me. I'll go to him, you'll see."

"You'll stay in your room until Doug takes you back to America." John spoke calmly, in command of himself with a practical solution at hand.

"You can't do this to me. I'm not a child."

"Then stop behaving like one." He gave a last instruction to the man and went off without glancing up again.

Noel slammed the window down. This was ridiculous. He'd have to let her out in the morning.

And then what? One or the other would be with her all the time. She felt something very like despair. Why did Jonas have to come at that moment? Had he watched her with Doug in Florida? A whole month and he'd been close by. She flung herself on the bed and closed her eyes.

Sleep overtook her unawares. She was awake again suddenly. The house was silent but something had wakened her. She sat up. Her door was ajar.

She glanced at her watch. Six in the morning.

Who had opened the door? Had it been that which had wakened her?

She went cautiously across the room and opened the door fully. The house was in darkness. She crept down the stairs. This time she'd get the torch. She edged into John's office and groped her way to the desk. The torch was where she had replaced it.

She picked it up and was halfway out of the room when she heard a wheezing kind of rattling breath behind her. She dropped the torch in fright and stood petrified as it was repeated.

Someone or something was in this room with her. She ducked down, searching for the heavy torch and then finding it clasped it nervously in front of her, shooting the beam wildly round the room.

She didn't expect to see John stretched out on the couch with a blanket over him. Her fingers snapped the torch out instinctively. Keeping guard ready for the first alert from the dogs. Typical. And he'd not even stirred with the light on his face.

She edged to the door, smiling a little and then turned again slowly. It was a very odd kind of snore.

She put the torch on again and this time she saw it—the dark red stain on the grey blanket, the glint of something silver.

She snapped on the main light. His eyes were closed, his face ashen, one hand trailed on the floor.

"Holy Mother of God!" Sharon stood in the doorway, her eyes wide with horror. "John!"

She ran towards him, stumbling a little. "John! Oh, John!"

She betrayed herself completely in that utterance. It wasn't Sharon, the maid, the girl who had helped her, who turned to face Noel. It was a woman seeing her man dead and her eyes were filled with an accusing hate that would have seared through metal. "Wasn't Christina enough for you? Why John? Oh, why John?"

8

"DON'T touch him," Noel said sharply, as Sharon turned away, her hand going to the knife. "He's still alive." She picked up the phone and dialled 999. Her voice was shaky as she asked for an ambulance and then the police.

Sharon stared at her. "Were you going to watch him die? Did I get up too early for you?"

"Why should I kill John?" Noel said tonelessly.

"Why did you kill Christina? They were both stopping you from getting what you wanted."

Noel shook her head wearily. "I didn't have to kill to get what I want. Stay with him. The ambulance shouldn't be long."

"Where are you going?" Sharon demanded sharply.

"I expect the police will find me easily enough." She walked out of the room, drawing back the bolts on the front door. She heard the ambulance siren when she was halfway across the brook.

She trudged through the woods. If she hadn't quarrelled with John would he still be alive? Had someone been waiting for that to happen? Ever since the dinner party? She'd recognised the knife at once. The little silver fruit knife Nicola had been so concerned about. It would have her fingerprints on it. There didn't seem to be any doubt about that.

She walked around to the front of the manor. She had to knock twice. A man opened the door, unshaven, tousled and in a woollen dressing gown. He knew who she was. She saw that at once by the widening of his eyes as she asked for Jonas.

Woodenly he asked her to wait and she sat in the hall, her eyes straying to the balustrades. She could see the break now, the splintered rails, the broken banister.

Jonas came swiftly, tying the belt of a dark green dressing gown. He looked as if he'd not slept for days and the dark stubble on his face emphasised his pallor.

He stopped a few feet away from her. "You shouldn't have come here."

"This time no one will be able to blame you," she said. "Dogs at the back, bolts on the doors and John guarding the stairs. No one could have got in from outside."

"What are you talking about?" he demanded. He'd not stopped to put anything on his feet. She stared at them. They were nice feet, long and narrow with straight toes. His pyjamas were dark green, too, but cotton, not silk like his dressing gown.

"I must look awful," she said. "I didn't take my make-up off last night and my hair . . ." Her hands went to it despairingly and Jonas took a step forward. "Noel, what's wrong?"

"Oh? Didn't I tell you? Someone tried to kill John last night. They'll blame me. I know they will. And you'll think I did it too, won't you? You thought I'd killed Christina. I came to tell you I didn't do it. And I didn't kill Christina either. It all happened like I said."

"I think you'd better come in here. Sam!" His shout was loud enough to wake the dead. She shuddered at the thought. "Make some coffee." He steered her into a little book-lined room and pushed her into a deep leather chair, switching on an electric fire and drawing it up in front of her.

"Now tell me." He pulled up a footstool and sat in front of her, chafing her hands. "You're frozen. Why didn't you put a coat on and some gloves?"

"The police might have stopped me if I'd lingered. I sent for them but Sharon was there. It won't be a sign in my favour. They'll say I had no choice. Why did you go away last night? Why didn't you wait for me?"

"You know why. He's in love with you. Now talk sense."

"I'm cold. And my head aches. It must be all that champagne I had last night." She blinked hard, putting her hand to her head. Jonas spoke to her but his voice sounded like a distant murmur. "I think I'm going to faint," she announced to her utmost surprise. "But I've never fainted in my life. I can't—"

The stinging, eye-watering smell of pungent smelling salts brought her round and she opened her eyes and saw Lady Valerie bending over her. She coughed, drawing back involuntarily. It was clearing her mind like a violent wind racing through her head.

Jonas was standing behind his mother.

"I must go," she said, struggling to get to her feet. "They mustn't find me here."

"You'll stay right where you are." Lady

Valerie pushed her back firmly. "When did you last eat?"

"Well, I had some lunch yesterday. I think," she added doubtfully. She couldn't remember eating a thing.

"Porridge," Lady Valerie announced. "Jonas go and tell Sam to make some right away, with lots of cream and sugar. And have a shave. No wonder the poor girl fainted. A horrible sight like that is enough to make anyone feel weak at the knees. And don't you say a word." She placed her finger across Noel's parted lips. "Not until you've eaten. Sam's porridge would bring fresh heart to anyone."

The warm kindness bestowed on her so naturally and spontaneously was almost too much to bear. She choked over the porridge but she did feel better once it was down and the creamy hot chocolate that followed completed the job of making her feel more like herself again.

"There's a good colour in your cheeks now," Lady Valerie said in approval. "And so we'll talk. Or perhaps . . ." She glanced at Jonas who had dressed as well as shaved and was sitting smoking on the other side of the room. "Perhaps you'd prefer me to leave you two alone." She nodded to herself. "Yes, I think you would," and, patting Noel's knee kindly, she murmured, "I never did like Christina. No heart! No heart at all. You'll do very well in her place."

"That's as good as the royal assent," Jonas murmured as his mother closed the door behind her. "Now that she's growing old she says exactly what she thinks. A prerogative of age she says."

"What have you told her?"

"I don't have to spell things out to my mother. We think alike."

"Then does she also think that I killed Christina?"

He threw his cigarette into the fireplace. "It would have been such an easy thing to do. And you thought the same of me. Admit it. Why say you heard me drive up? That worried you, didn't it? And the lift going. Why didn't you tell me about that?"

"I was going to, that night. Then I forgot. Why didn't they arrest you?"

"There were too many things that couldn't be explained. Powell doesn't like loose ends. Now what's this about John?"

She told him, quietly this time, and sensibly,

and he frowned when she'd finished. "So that leaves Rosemary or Nicola in the running and of the two I think I'd plump for Nicola. She's been an opportunist all her life. She was friendly with Christina, she was in and out of this house. She could have been here that day. Christina could have told her what she was going to do. And Rosemary would not have had the same opportunities for getting a photograph of me to put in the locket. She was only here a couple of times."

"But Nicola can't hate me. She scarcely knows me."

"I'll tell you something about Nicola. She—" He paused. "No, perhaps not."

"You needn't be modest. No doubt she fancies her chances with you, but I think she's like that with any presentable male. She is certainly all over Doug."

"Ah, yes, Douglas Brominsky." He frowned. "I found out a lot about him."

"And left me to him. No one will believe you were in Florida all that time and you didn't even come up and say hello."

"Believe me, staying away from you then was the hardest thing I ever did in my whole life. I was within ten yards of you once. I had to know

192

you were all right. When John told me you'd disappeared I could have throttled him. Anything could have happened to you and he didn't seem to care. He wouldn't go to the police, he wouldn't do anything. So I did something about it, a little too late in the day to find you before you went to America but once found it was easy enough to keep track of you. Do you mind?"

"I mind your keeping silent. You could have written."

"No. I had nothing to offer you and you were making a new life for yourself. It would have been criminal to interfere."

"And now?"

"And now I wonder if you know your own mind."

"I wouldn't have thought you would ever need reassurance on that point."

"Last night . . ."

"Oh, last night," she said impatiently. "You read something into the way we were dancing that was supposed to be for other people's benefit. The whole family was determined to show that I couldn't be involved in Christina's death. With Dr. Shepherd aiding and abetting and Doug acting the part in earnest, they had me almost married off to him on the spot. Then you showed up and it was all for nothing. Why did you come?"

"I thought you'd be worried."

"And there I was—dancing, laughing, enjoying myself and in the arms of another man. Next time don't run away. Make your claim instead."

"My claim?"

"You do intend to make one, I hope. After all, your mother has approved."

A little smile appeared on his lips, lightening his whole face. "Don't rush me. First of all I think the police have a prior claim. I'll take you to the station before they come here for you."

Noel sighed resignedly. "Patience is not a virtue I admire but I suppose you're right."

"I'll telephone and say we're on our way." He went into another room to do it and Noel borrowed a comb and went to the cloakroom for a wash and brush up.

There was no waiting at the police station this time. They were shown straight up into Powell's office. Watkins was with him but there was no uniformed man to take down notes. They listened to what she had to say in silence, making no comment about Nicola.

"I know there's no proof," she said, "but it has to be one or the other and Nicola had the better opportunities."

"Not necessarily so. There were three more people in the house last night."

"Three?"

"Mrs. Cassell, Miss Torrence and Mr. Brominsky."

"Miss Torrence? Oh, Sharon! She wouldn't have tried to kill John. She—"

"Yes?" He waited expectantly.

"Well, she wouldn't." She couldn't betray Sharon's love. Maybe no one else knew about it—not even John. "She was horrified when she saw him."

"She made a statement to the police. She accused you of killing him—and of killing Mrs. Fenton. She handed over some clothing of yours."

"Then she did me a favour. It will prove that strand of wool doesn't match."

"But it does—at least on a cursory examination. It's with the labs now."

"But if it matches then that means it was taken earlier, before I was wearing it."

Powell glanced at a list he extracted from a file on his desk. "You brought with you two pairs of slacks, two sweaters—one thick knit and one lambswool, a suit, two long dresses and a trouser suit? It wouldn't take much imagination to guess what you would wear. I think you'll find a strand of wool missing from the lambswool sweater as well."

"You mean you know, don't you?"

"We did notice it."

"So that's why you let me go?"

"It was a part of it. A part of why we didn't hold either of you. Of course, there is always the possibility that you took care of that yourself. It wouldn't be the first time a guilty person has arranged a clumsy frame to prove his innocence."

"But you don't believe that," she said, trying for confidence and failing miserably.

"I wouldn't care to say what we believed at this moment, Miss Clare, but thank you for coming in to see us. We have some more checking to do but we'll be talking to you again."

"They don't think it's Nicola," Noel said in the car.

"I don't know," Jonas said heavily. "Shall we go to the hospital?"

She nodded, but John was in the intensive care unit. They weren't allowed to see him.

"Will he be all right?" Noel asked.

The nurse lifted her shoulders. "He's lost a lot of blood but the knife missed the heart. He could pull through."

"Has he come round at all?"

"Not that I know of. His wife is with him now. Shall I tell her you're here?"

"No. It doesn't matter." Jonas took Noel's arm. "We'll go through her room," he said once they were out of earshot of the nurse. "We won't get a better opportunity."

"And what are we looking for? She'll not have left anything lying around."

"You never know." He drove to the farmhouse at a speed that paid no heed to current regulations, but searching Nicola's room was not such an easy job.

First Rosemary appeared, greeting Jonas eagerly and insisting that he had coffee, and then Doug showed up and joined them, his usual politeness trimmed with icy hostility as the introductions were made.

Noel left them exchanging barbed words, with Rosemary as mediator, and went upstairs but Sharon was there to block her way.

"I've told the police everything," she said defiantly. "You won't get away with it. And I gave them your bloodstained clothes. They'll not be long in coming for you now."

"You did the right thing, Sharon," Noel said gently.

"I did?" Sharon took a step backwards, her eyes wary and suspicious.

"Of course you did. I've only just left the police station. As a matter of fact, you did me a favour."

"You're lying. It's a trick to get me off my guard. But I'm ready for you. I've been waiting for you to come back." She turned and snatched up something from underneath the bow-fronted chest of drawers on the landing.

It was Noel's turn to take a step backwards. She was holding John's shotgun.

"Now you are going to walk down those stairs and wait until the police get here," she said jerkily. "And don't think I won't fire it. I thought a lot of John."

"Yes, Sharon, I know," Noel said soothingly. "And you're very upset and you're not thinking straight. Now just be careful with that thing." Would Sharon have known how to load it? She decided not to take the chance of finding out.

"John's going to get better," she said. "He's lost a lot of blood but the knife missed the heart."

"I ought to kill you now," Sharon said. "People like you aren't fit to live. So they'll shut you up for a few years but then they'll let you out and you'll try to kill the first persons that stands in your way again."

"No, Sharon, I won't. I mean I didn't do it." Noel backed rapidly as Sharon advanced and stumbled on the first stair. She grabbed for the banister and felt her weak ankle turn on her.

"Standing over him and watching his life drain away," Sharon said, her eyes wide and staring. She wasn't seeing Noel. She was caught up in her own private nightmare.

"I know you're in love with him," Noel said desperately, "but there is really no need to go to such extremes. Do, please, phone the police." She hopped down to the next stair.

"Don't try to smooth talk me again. I liked you. I actually *liked* you. And you could do this to John."

"I tell you I didn't do it," Noel shouted. What were they doing downstairs? Couldn't they hear what was going on?

"I thought I'd get up early and take him a

cup of tea and I saw that light bobbing in the room. I knew right away something was wrong. John! My poor John!" The gun wavered dangerously in her hands.

Noel hit the bottom stair before she expected it and turned her ankle again. This time it gave way under her and she fell in an undignified heap.

"Just what do you think you're doing, Sharon?" Rosemary said in a voice that rang with authority. "Put that silly thing down and get on with your work."

"She killed John," Sharon said dully, not taking her eyes from Noel.

"Stuff and nonsense. Noel wouldn't harm a fly." Rosemary stepped round Noel and marched firmly up the stairs to where Sharon was standing. "Give me that at once."

Sharon blinked and shook her head and Rosemary's hand went smartly across her face. Left, right. The smack of it made Noel wince.

Sharon must have seen stars. Her eyes rolled and Rosemary grasped the shotgun and pulled.

Noel shut her eyes, cringing in anticipation of the blast, but when she opened them again Rosemary was leading Sharon down the stairs, the shotgun hanging loosely in her own hand.

"Put it away," she said to Noel, and dropped it carelessly in her lap. "I'll have to see to Sharon. She's upset."

"*She's* upset." Doug let his breath out in a long sigh. Both the men were standing frozen in the doorway of the sitting room. "I don't mind admitting I was scared half out of my mind. I thought that girl would let fly at the least sign of opposition."

"I think she would have done if anyone else had made a move," Jonas assured him. He shook himself and came forward to help Noel to her feet.

"What a girl," Doug said, staring after Rosemary. "Nerves of steel."

"Not like me," Noel said wryly. She limped to the office, snapping the gun open. It was loaded, both barrels. She quivered at the thought and put it away quickly.

"I'll take another look at that ankle," Jonas said. "I think you've really wrenched it this time."

"I'll survive—that at least." She lowered her voice. "I didn't get the chance to look. Sharon stopped me on the landing."

"I'll go. Doug!" He took her arm and said,

"I think this little lady needs a drink after that experience."

"Don't we all, boy. Don't we all!" Doug already had the Scotch out. "That girl," he said. "She knew exactly what to do. Marvellous!" He shook his head in admiration.

Noel felt like saying it was easy to be brave when you didn't care very much if the person at the wrong end of the gun got hit or not, but she bit back the sour retort. Rosemary *had* kept her head and acted in the only way Sharon would accept.

Jonas excused himself and more of a way of holding Doug there than in further extolling Rosemary's virtues she began to talk about her, remembering the time when she had saved one of the village children from drowning when they'd been skating on the pond and the ice had given way. Then there was the time when she'd spotted a light in one of the cottages when she'd known the owners were away. She'd promptly called the police and they'd caught a burglar. "She's wasting her life now," Noel said. "It's no wonder she's unhappy. My mother wouldn't want her to wave her youth goodbye, but she's the only person who can look after her properly."

Rosemary came in rubbing her eyes. She sounded deathly tired. "Mrs. Cassell's taken over. What an extraordinary thing for Sharon to do!"

"She's in love with John. Didn't you know?"

"With John!" She blinked and murmured, "How very odd. It must amuse Nicola."

"She can't know. She wouldn't keep Sharon on if she had any idea of it."

"Oh, Noel." Rosemary shook her head wearily. "Haven't you fathomed out the way Nicola's mind works yet? She likes to have a hold over people. She enjoys the sense of power it gives her. I heard what you were saying to Doug and I know she told you she'd wanted to get a nurse in for Mother but she likes me here. She likes me to be dependent on her charity. Is that Scotch you're drinking? I'd like one, too —a large one. Lunch is going to be late today. Is Jonas staying? Where is he?"

"No, we won't be staying. I'm taking Noel out." Jonas gave a slight shake of the head to the enquiry in Noel's eyes and stepped through the doorway.

The hostility between the two men seemed to have vanished. Jonas had a drink and then bore Noel off without Doug even attempting to raise an objection. He was too busy refilling Rose-mary's glass. After the first drink a flush had come to her cheeks and she had started to look more cheerful.

"Wouldn't it be nice if he could fall in love with Rosemary?" Noel said in the car.

"He's certainly bowled over at the moment." Jonas laughed at her. "What a tidy mind you have. How do you want to see it end? Rosemary with Doug, Sharon with John—"

"And you with me." She reached for his hand. "Especially you with me."

"We've waited long enough." Jonas covered her hand for a moment and then abruptly started the car. "I don't want you to go back to the farm. I don't think it's safe for you."

"I couldn't come to the manor, not now. It's too soon, and it will look bad."

"I can move out. My mother will look after you."

"It's not that. I mean it makes no difference whether you're there or not. It's your home. I'll have to wait until everything is cleared up and everyone knows I didn't kill Christina."

"The police can't act without proof. Supposing they never get it?"

"I think they will." She stared out of the window. "What did her first husband die of?"

"That's an idea," Jonas said thoughtfully. "It might not be her first time in getting rid of someone."

"Marion and Barry would know. Let's go to lunch at 'The Ship'. They seem to sit there every day."

But they were not at "The Ship." It was crowded with Sunday drinkers and they ate quickly, finding out from the receptionist where the Nevilles lived.

It was one of the pretty-pretty cottages on the outskirts of the town; a thatched roof, brilliantly painted shutters, latticed windows and roses climbing up the white walls.

They knocked at the door and Marion opened it, her ugly mannish face reflecting her surprise. "Well, well! We are honoured," she said ironically. "Come in. Join us for a drink. Sunday is my day for wrestling with the devil in the form of our kitchen stove and I need a lot of Dutch courage to face it."

They stepped down straight into the living room, a glorious confusion of bold modern furniture and the clutter of ages. The Sunday newspapers were scattered on the floor, a wreath of cigarette smoke hung low like a cloud, a wealth of bottles littered the table. Barry was typing at a table near the fire, surrounded by half-open books, sheets of manuscript and overflowing ashtrays. A huge black cat was sleeping on his lap, apparently undisturbed by his typing. An ominous smell of burning came from the kitchen; an American styled streamlined annexe to the main room separated from it by an open-latticed framework.

"My God! The potatoes! And I've only just put them on." Marion rushed to the stove and jerked the pan off the ring, swearing as the handle burned her. "They're all right," she muttered. "It won't taste." And she opened the oven door and turned the pan over a tray of sizzling fat, screaming as it splashed up.

Barry rose, throwing the cat on a chair, his wife's mutters and screams such a matter of indifference to him that Noel could only assume it was a normal event for her to burn herself.

"Nice to see you," he said affably. "We don't get many visitors on a Sunday. Marion is not her usual self. What'll you have? I think we've got pretty well everything."

Looking at the array of bottles Noel saw no

reason to doubt his boast. She had a sherry and Jonas a beer. Marion came back to clear a space on the settee for them, cheerfully dumping the stuff she gathered from it on the floor at the side. "Now what can we do for you?" she asked, filling a tumbler half full of gin and adding a drop of angostura. "I take it this isn't a social call?"

Noel glanced at Jonas uncomfortably but as it didn't seem a subject that could be reached by any amount of small talk she said bluntly, "Can you tell us how Nicola's first husband died?"

"Why? What's happened now?" Marion didn't seem at all perturbed by the question, but Barry sat very still.

"There was an attempt on John's life last night."

"I see." Marion sipped from the glass, her gaze going from Jonas to Noel thoughtfully. "And of course Nicola's the outsider—the foreigner like us—and as such a suspect. She had no reason to kill John. *She* has the money in that marriage."

"But she didn't have the money in her first, did she?"

"It was a natural death. He had cancer. Don't

207

look to Nicola for a convenient way of getting out of the mess you've made for yourself." She set down her glass so hard some of the contents slopped over. "And you come to us! Her friends! What kind of people do you think we are? Get out of here."

Noel put down her sherry glass. Jonas had already risen. "I'm sorry if you feel we've insulted you," he said quietly. "We didn't mean it that way."

He opened the door for Noel and they walked up the flagged path to the car.

Before they'd entered it, however, Barry came out of the cottage. Jonas paused but it was at Noel Barry addressed his remark. "He didn't have cancer," he said. "He only believed he had. They said at the inquest that he took his own life while the balance of his mind was disturbed. Phenobarbitone it was. Nicola had been sleeping very badly."

9

"**H**E thinks she did it," Noel said as they were driving away.

"And that settles it. You're not going back to the farm."

"Yes, I must . . . for a little longer. Don't be afraid for me, Jonas. Nicola doesn't scare me. Will you take me to Dr. Shepherd's? I think I'd like him to look at this ankle."

"Is it hurting?"

"Just a little," she said with truth, but it wasn't her ankle she was thinking about. She told him to wait in the car, she wouldn't be a moment and, exaggerating her limp, she went in to see the doctor and told him what she wanted.

"You're playing a foolish game," he said. "What do you hope to achieve by that?"

"It might provide some sort of proof."

"How?"

"Well, I've not worked out the details yet," she admitted blithely. "But you'll make that phone call, won't you?"

"I don't know that I will. Does Jonas know about this? No, of course he doesn't. He'd never allow you to do it. Don't you realise, Noel, that if you're right, Nicola is a very dangerous woman?"

"I tell you what I do realise. Unless this is cleared up I'll never be able to marry Jonas and live at the manor. You must know what that would mean to Jonas. This is his home, where he belongs, and it's my home, too. I've been away a long time and I know what such an exile is like. You can help me or I'll do it alone. No one is going to stop me."

He chewed his lip indecisively and she said with a quick change of tone, "Will you bind up my ankle while I'm here? I've given it a bit of a wrench."

"Look at you," he said in exasperation. "Just look at you. Your face, your arm, and now your ankle. You're not safe to be left alone anywhere. I've never met anyone more accident prone."

She smiled beguilingly at him. "I always survive though."

"There's a first time for everything," he said gloomily. "Sugar pills! What next? I'll be some time."

He went into his surgery and returned with

a small bottle. "Ten," he said. "One only to be taken at bedtime."

"Put 'Danger' on the label, too," Noel prompted as he wrote in his tiny crabbed hand on the bottle.

"Caution is the word," he said. "And that's how I hope you'll play it. So you're distraught and half out of your mind with the worry of it all. You're sure that everyone believes you're a murderer and I've suddenly become suspicious of your asking me for sleeping pills. I tell Nicola to make sure you don't take an overdose. It's crazy," he finished flatly.

"If she tries to kill me with them it won't be so crazy. Think how convenient it would be for her. The scene all set for a suicide. She won't be able to resist it. And then when she thinks I'm nodding off for ever I'll get her talking, tape every word and hey presto . . . It's much neater and easier than trying to frame me for murder."

"Supposing the tape machine doesn't work?"

"I'll get two. Blow the extravagance." She lifted her foot. "Now my ankle."

Jonas was walking up the path when she and the doctor appeared at the door. "I was beginning to think you'd whipped her off to hospital for X-rays," he said. "What's the verdict?"

"A slight strain; it's a little swollen. She shouldn't do anything strenuous in the next few days. Jonas—"

"Thanks, doctor," Noel cut in, a dangerous glint in her eyes.

"I really do feel that—"

"That I'm asking for trouble. I know. It's always been the way. I promise to keep it up on a velvet cushion as soon as I get home. Come on, Jonas. Goodbye, Dr. Shepherd."

She took Jonas by the hand and led him firmly down the path.

The doctor made no further attempt to tell Jonas what she planned to do. He stood at the doorway watching them depart and then, as she lifted her hand to wave goodbye, turned decisively and went back inside.

She felt a moment's unease and then dismissed it and asked Jonas to take her back into Elmsbury.

"I'll take you anywhere you like," he said agreeably. "But why Elmsbury?"

"I want to do some shopping."

"On a Sunday?"

She stared at him in dismay. She'd forgotten

that and then her mind started working again. Barry was almost certain to have a tape recorder. He might lend it to her—if she could ask him without Marion knowing.

"I've just remembered something I should have asked the doctor to do," she said hurriedly. "Hang on a moment."

She didn't bother to knock but went right in. The doctor was just replacing the telephone receiver on its rest. She stared at him suspiciously. "Who were you phoning?"

"The hospital." He smiled blandly. "Who else? Can you blame me for wondering?"

She didn't like that bland smile. "You were trying to tell Jonas. I thought doctors were like priests. A confidence is sacred."

"And so it is," he assured her. "Absolutely sacred. You'll be glad to know John is out of danger."

"Did you speak to Nicola?"

"No. She's on her way home."

"Has John said anything?"

"I don't know. It wasn't the sort of thing I could ask."

"No, I suppose not." She opened the telephone directory and looked up the Nevilles' number. "May I use your phone?"

"Be my guest."

Barry answered. He listened to her request and then said flatly, "Yes, I've got one. You can borrow it."

"Could you—"

"I'll leave it at 'The Ship' with the receptionist," he interrupted brusquely. "I don't want to know why you want it and I don't want anyone asking questions. I suppose that suits you?"

"Yes, Barry. Thank you. It's—"

She was talking to herself. He'd cut the connection. She replaced the receiver slowly. He'd guessed why she wanted it, of course.

"So that's one," Dr. Shepherd said, getting out his pipe and unfolding his tobacco pouch. "Where are you going to get the other one from?"

"I don't suppose you've got one?"

"No, I have not. You'd forgotten it was Sunday, hadn't you? I wonder how many other things you've not taken into account?"

"Don't be an old fusspot." She leaned forward and kissed his cheek impulsively. "You can call me tomorrow to make sure I'm still alive and kicking."

"John's out of danger," she told Jonas. "Isn't that wonderful?"

"It's good news certainly," Jonas agreed. "But it means Nicola will be leaving the hospital."

"Oh, let's not bother about Nicola any more this afternoon. Let's just forget about everything but ourselves. When shall we get married, for instance? And where shall we go for our honeymoon?"

Jonas laughed, and she managed to keep him laughing during the rest of the afternoon, but as she waved him goodbye she felt an acute sense of desolation and loss. He hadn't wanted to leave her but she had insisted, convincing him that Nicola would be too well satisfied with what she had done already to risk spoiling her delicate groundwork for the frame. Only when the police showed no signs of arresting her would she try something else. Until then she would be safe. Jonas had seen the logic of that. He never thought for a moment she would be stupid enough to risk forcing Nicola's hand. And maybe she wouldn't. Maybe her nerve would fail her.

She walked slowly into the farmhouse by the back way.

Sharon was dicing some vegetables. She paused in her task, her hand tightening around the handle of the knife. Her eyes had shrunk to little bloodshot balls beneath the puffed and swollen lids. She looked terrible.

Noel felt a queasy feeling in her stomach but it had to be faced. "Well?" she said.

"If John dies, I will kill you," Sharon said tonelessly. The very flatness of her tone was far more frightening than any passionate declaration would have been.

Noel took a deep breath, running her tongue over suddenly dry lips. "But he's not going to die."

"That's not what *she* said," Mrs. Cassell said from the pantry doorway. "She's just left him."

"And she said what? Her exact words, please."

Mrs. Cassell considered her dispassionately, much as if she were looking at a total stranger for the very first time. "She told us to pray— only a miracle could save him now."

"I don't believe it. Dr. Shepherd said he was out of danger. Ring the hospital. They'll tell you."

"Mrs. Clare is sitting by the telephone right now, expecting them to tell her to get back to the hospital as quickly as possible. She fears the worst. It's written all over her."

"It's a put on. Haven't you got the wit to see that? She wants you to believe that; she wants us all to believe it; she wants—" What did she want? What was she working up to now? Or could it be true? Had John had a relapse?

"Get your coat," she said abuptly to Sharon. "I want you to come with me to the hospital. And if Nicola wants to know where we are," she turned to Mrs. Cassell, "you've not seen me and you've given Sharon an hour off. All right?"

Sharon hadn't moved. Mrs. Cassell nodded slowly. "Go with her, Sharon. It can't do any harm."

"Unless you think, of course, that I have plans for seeing you off on the way! But if you feel like that, Sharon, bring that knife along. You can use it at the first suspicious move I make."

Sharon said nothing. She stared at Noel and then dropped her eyes to the knife. For a good few seconds she remained motionless.

Noel said quietly, "I thought you were going to kill me this afternoon, Sharon. Do you think

I'd risk being alone with you now unless I was sure I could prove my point? Come with me."

"All right. I will." Sharon considered the knife a moment more and then put it down dully, wiping her hands on her apron before taking it off and going for her coat.

"You'll have to take the Landrover," Mrs. Cassell said. "Your American friend has got your sister-in-law's car. He's taken Rosemary out in it."

"Good for him." Noel met Mrs. Cassell's steady gaze and, with a sense of shock, realised that while Mrs. Cassell might be reserving judgement there was enough doubt in her mind to make her consider her capable of murder. It wouldn't be so hard to convince Nicola that she thought everyone believed her guilty for Nicola must know already what Sharon and Mrs. Cassell were thinking.

Sharon didn't speak once on the way to the hospital. She sat hunched up in her seat, pressing her folded arms against herself as if hugging a pain.

Noel made no attempt to get her to talk. She drove with deep concentration. Pray! She was praying all right and someone, somewhere, must have heard her. Of course it had been a

218

silly thought that Nicola would have tried some-thing at the hospital. She wouldn't have had a chance. A policeman was in the room and a nurse was in constant attendance. "He's not going to die, is he?" Noel said fiercely. The fight to get in to see him had been a gruelling one.

The nurse shook her head and Noel turned to Sharon. "You see," she said triumphantly. But Sharon wasn't listening, wasn't even looking at her. She was gazing at John, who had opened his eyes and was looking at her as if he were seeing a vision.

"I'll wait outside in the car for you," Noel said hurriedly.

"No, don't bother. I'll find my own way back." Sharon moved towards the bedside with a springy confidence in her step, smiling through the tears which had welled up in her eyes.

"You're crying over me?" John demanded incredulously.

"Of course not." She sat down, wiping her cheeks with the back of her hand. "I think I must have a cold. How do you feel? You had us worried for a while."

"Us? Or just you, Sharon?"

Noel thought it prudent to retire at that point. She went to "The Ship" and picked up the tape recorder Barry had left for her. It was a neat piece of extravagance, small enough to fit into her handbag.

She worked out how it operated and went. back to the farm. "I left Sharon at the hospital," she said, answering the question that rushed to Mrs. Cassell's eyes as she walked in alone. "And John is just fine and responding with some surprise but immense gratification to Sharon's concern. Has Nicola been in here?"

"She's not stirred from her sitting room, not even to change for dinner. That's not like her. She must be worried sick."

"Oh, of course. After all, she loved him, didn't she? Really loved him. It was touching to see them together. What's the matter with you, Mrs. Cassell? You can doubt me—whom you've known from childhood—and yet you even refuse to consider her as a candidate for the role you've cast for me."

"She had no reason," Mrs. Cassell said, flushing deeply.

"And *I* did. And everyone will think the same." She slammed the door behind her. The act that was no longer an act was in its first scene.

Nicola was huddled up in a chair staring into the fire, with only one light from a small table lamp burning. "Oh, it's you," she said without enthusiasm as Noel walked in. "Dr. Shepherd called. He was worried about you."

"Are you sure he wasn't worried about you? Being in the same house as me, that is? Did he tell you to lock your door at night and lock away all the knives?"

"Don't be silly," Nicola said, but it was an automatic response that held no conviction.

"You think I did it, too, don't you?" Noel said bitterly, "What did John say? That he knew it was me?"

"He hasn't come round at all. He's going to die. Does that please you, Noel? There's no one in the way of your marrying Jonas now. The only trouble is that the police have applied for a warrant for your arrest. They'll be here in the morning."

Noel narrowed her eyes. It should have been very satisfying that Nicola was falling into the pattern of behaviour she had predicted, but there was something off key, something that made her uneasy. She was the manipulator, she was the cat in this cat and mouse game and yet Nicola was playing her part as if anticipating what Noel wanted her to say next. It was her imagination, it had to be. "Why are you telling me this?" she said slowly.

"I thought you might want to make the most of your last night of freedom. Why don't you ring Jonas and ask him to come over? Or is Jonas being wary? Is he wondering whether he's fallen out of the frying pan into the fire? It can't be very pleasant to reflect on what will happen when you have your first row or if you suddenly decide you've had enough of marriage. He might be relieved when you are arrested. He won't marry you then even if a miracle does happen and the jury let you go. Jonas is very proud of his family name."

Noel stared at her and then turned abruptly and rushed out of the room.

She was sitting on the edge of the bed, the bottle of sugar pills in her hand when Nicola followed.

"I'll take those," Nicola said briskly, suiting action to words. "We can't have you killing yourself and cheating the public of the trial. They'll want to know all the details of your private life, they'll drag it all out. Poor Jonas.

He's going to be right in the thick of it. People will want to know what it is about him that could drive a woman to kill."

Noel buried her face in her hands. "I didn't do it. I didn't do it."

"You'll never be able to prove it," Nicola said very softly. "There will always be that doubt in people's minds. I'll tell you what I'll do. I'll leave these here. I'll tell Dr. Shepherd I couldn't find them."

Noel dropped her hands and raised her head slowly. "No. That's not the way. If I kill myself people will have no doubt at all then. I can't do that. I have to fight."

Nicola smiled. "I had an idea you might say that. Very well then . . . fight—right to the bitter end. Now come and eat. Dinner must be ready now."

Mrs. Cassell served the meal but Nicola made no comment on Sharon's absence. She played with the food on her plate, barely eating. Noel ate stolidly. The scene was set now for the last act. Nicola would appear in her room as she was going to bed, she would press on her a milk drink and in it would be the sugar pills. It had to be like that. She had failed to make her kill herself. She must realise she had to do the job herself.

She spent half an hour with her mother and then went to her room. The tape recorder was under the bed, all set for action. She got into bed and waited.

Nicola came earlier than she had expected. The drink was in a tall beaker on a tray. She set it down on the bedside table. There was one pill on the napkin. "One only," Nicola said. "As per Dr. Shepherd's instructions. You'll sleep tonight."

Noel picked up the pill, put it on her tongue and lifted the beaker to her lips. She swallowed it down. Sugar pills indeed. The doctor had allowed his sense of humour to get the better of him. Maybe he thought it would teach her a lesson. The drink tasted horrible. She drained the beaker and set it down, flopping back on the pillow, her hand going over the other side of the bed to switch on the tape recorder.

"It's odd how things turn out," Nicola said musingly. "This time last week I was hardly aware of your existence. If I thought of you at all I equated you with Rosemary—just another moonstruck kid too hidebound to do anything that could possibly bring censure on your head.

Poor Rosemary. She really is pathetic. She'll never get anything she wants. She doesn't scheme or fight or use other people. She waits and hopes, knowing that time is running out, making it more and more certain that she'll never get out of the prison she's made for herself. You should have seen her face when I made Doug take her out to dinner, hating me for it yet unable to resist the temptation. She'll be stammering and stuttering and saying all the wrong things, conscious all the time that whatever progress she makes I can spoil it all with just a few words when she returns. I like Doug but of course he bears no comparison with Jonas. I've had my eye on him for a long time."

"And found him more than a match for you."

"I wouldn't say that," Nicola said mockingly. "Circumstances have been against it. It will be different now. Your arrival was most opportune and I saw at once how you could be used. A dream is almost impossible to vanquish but once it materialises it's easy enough to shatter and send rolling in the dust. I don't foresee any opposition from Jonas. He'll be only too glad of someone capable of understanding, someone who can give him comfort when his dream has crumbled before his eyes. I rather fancy myself as the lady of the manor. Christina was terribly hard to bear at times although it was easy enough to manipulate her into doing what I wanted."

"Was that scene at the dinner table your doing?"

"But of course. Christina couldn't laugh at you as she did at Rosemary. You were someone to be feared. You wouldn't be content with a few kind words and an occasional chance meeting. You'd gone further than that before John sent you away. Your return was a danger signal she couldn't overlook, especially when you lost no time in picking up the threads. I had great pleasure in telling her about your night out. It was easy enough to make her believe he'd stayed with you at 'The Ship'. I knew how she'd react to that. She'd been too successful with Jonas to doubt that the threat of taking her own life wouldn't work in getting her own way. All it required was a change in the setting. I was surprised when you fell for it. I thought you'd have been capable of watching her carry out her threat. She might have done it, you know. I was hoping she would. It's so much more satisfying to make people do the dirty work themselves. My first husband was very obliging in that respect. He was a hard man, violently jealous and almost impossible to deceive but he had a weakness. He was deathly afraid of illness and when he had to go into hospital for a very simple operation it was easy to convince him that in reality he had cancer. I even managed to cry as I described the pain and agony that lay ahead. I held his head as he took that fatal dose and when I was sure that he was dying I told him what a fool he'd been and what I really thought of him. I enjoyed that—seeing the fear and horror in his eyes and the knowledge that there wasn't a thing on earth he could do to save himself. How do you feel, Noel? Am I boring you? You look as if you're falling asleep."

Her smile was mocking, her words sardonic. Noel could picture her very easily at her dying husband's bedside. She hooded her eyes and slid further down in the bed but she didn't really have to pretend she was sleepy. It was becoming an effort to stay awake. The bed was too warm, she'd lost too much sleep the night before. Nicola's face drew her gaze like a magnet—the gloating triumph in her eyes, the cruel smile on her mouth. "John never knew. I had to do that in the dark. A knife isn't a weapon I'd use from choice but it was an incentive with your fingerprints on it and worth foregoing the pleasure of seeing the knowledge in his eyes. He guesses though. I saw that when he opened his eyes to see me waiting there at the hospital. The closeness of death sharpens the faculties. Christina realised what I was going to do without my having to say a word. She was so terrified she couldn't even shout for help."

Noel's gaze dropped to Nicola's hands. She was playing with the pill bottle. She heard the movement of the pills inside as she turned it over and over.

"Have I said enough to incriminate myself now?" Nicola asked mockingly. "Is this your moment of triumph? Or are you beginning to wonder why I am being so obliging? I see you are." She unscrewed the cap of the bottle and emptied the pills into the palm of her hand. "Nine pills—harmless, I imagine. Fortunately I had some phenobarbitone hidden away for just such an emergency as this. I prefer to use a tried and trusted formula—and you swallowed it like a lamb. Such a very predictable girl. It's been a pleasure to deal with you. Tomorrow I shall tell Dr. Shepherd that I did as he asked and made sure you didn't take more than one of the pills he gave you. I couldn't possibly have known you had an additional supply. I shall be desolate, quite desolate. I shall cry when I tell them how despondent you were and how I tried to cheer you up. But you have left a letter which explains everything. It's a very touching letter. They might even feel sorry for you. Allowing the love you feel for one man to drive you to such lengths and then overcome with conscience when you realise Jonas suspects what you have done for him."

"You'll never get away with it," Noel cried, trying to urge her limbs into motion. A deadly lethargy was binding her muscles and chaining her to the bed.

"I don't see why not. There's nothing around in your handwriting. Americans use the phone." Nicola rolled the pills back into the bottle and screwed the cap on again.

"Dr. Shepherd knows."

"You mean he listened to what you had to say. I can talk my way around that. It's only natural that you should try to throw suspicion on someone else. He won't be able to prove a thing. Now where's this tape recorder you've got going?"

She looked straight under the bed and

laughed. "As I said—so predictable! I think I would have guessed what you were up to even if Marion hadn't phoned and told me you'd been round asking questions. When she phoned again to tell me Barry had taken his tape recorder out with him I could have dictated the script for what followed." She moved around the bed and Noel lunged for the recording machine. Nicola beat her to it easily, whisking it away from her feebly groping fingers.

"I'm almost tempted to keep it," she said. "It would be interesting listening on a dull evening. However . . . safety first." She pressed the button for erase and Noel said dully, "Jonas will know."

"Not at all. You've not told him what you planned to do, that's obvious. He'd never have allowed it. And he's already afraid that you killed Christina. I shall have a delightful time consoling him. How are you feeling now, Noel? Limbs as heavy as lead, terribly, terribly sleepy? Why don't you try shouting for help?"

"Will anyone hear?"

"Your mother might. Of course, she can't exactly come rushing to help. And Mrs. Cassell is snoring her head off. I gave her a little pheno-barbitone, too, not enough to make her wonder but she won't be waking up until morning. You'll be cold by then, quite beyond help."

"There's Sharon."

"She's not in the house. Poor girl. There's another pathetic case for you. She'd give her soul for a chance of going into John's arms and he's not even got the wit to see it. She'll be crying in some corner now. I told her he was dying and she was quite cut up about it. I hear she almost killed you this afternoon, so I doubt if she'll come to your aid even if she knew you needed it. Everyone believes you did it. It will come as no surprise to anyone to find you've committed suicide."

"Rosemary and Doug will be back soon."

"Not before midnight. By then you'll be beyond speech. I know the stages. Already you are slurring your words and you couldn't get out of that bed if you tried. Have a go!"

Noel was filled with despair. She'd been out-manoeuvred like a child. Nicola was right. She couldn't move and her tongue felt swollen, her mouth as numb as if shot with novacaine.

Nicola laughed and said indulgently, "You didn't have a chance. I didn't plan your death —you brought this on yourself. All I wanted was Jonas and I to be free and you were a fine scapegoat—the *only* scapegoat. You had to be out of the way, too. But death is better—so much more final. Now I suppose I'd better check that you haven't left anything else around to point the finger at me." She moved around the room, looking in the wardrobe, going through the drawers, her suitcase, even lifting up the pillow.

Noel closed her eyes. There was no hope in her. Dr. Shepherd would suspect but what could he do? A lone voice in the village. The only one who hadn't considered her capable of killing Christina.

She barely noticed the cry from Nicola. Curiosity was dead. Nothing could affect her now. But she felt returning feeling as Nicola held her up, slapping her face from side to side. "What is it? Where does it go?"

"W-what?"

"This." Nicola flung her back on the pillows and ran to the window. She had pulled back the curtains. The window was open about an inch and a thin black wire went over the sill.

Noel stared at it without comprehension. It looked like a telephone wire. Or a television aerial. ˙

"Don't act dumb with me," Nicola screamed.

She dropped to her hands and knees and followed the wire. It fitted in between the edge of the carpet and the wall, invisible to an ordinary glance. The end of it was behind the headboard.

Nicola wrenched it out, staring with unconcealed fury at the minute microphone at the end of it. "The police," she breathed. "You bitch. You utter bitch. I never thought you had it in you. All right then—whoever's listening in— you put one step in this house and your precious little stoolpigeon is a goner for sure. I've got a gun. I'll blow her from here to kingdom come and the first one that comes in gets the same."

She pulled the microphone away from the wire and, opening the window wide, hurled it away into the darkness.

Noel reached weakly for a vase on the table as Nicola ran to the door. Pain. It was the only way to keep alive. She smashed the vase against the edge of the table and clenched the sharp edges of a piece of the shattered glass in her hand. The pain of it pierced through the lethargy that numbed her nerve centres, the clouds in her brain. She flopped out of the bed and crawled along the floor.

Nicola had vanished. Gritting her teeth, the glass grinding into her hand, Noel half fell and half rolled down the stairs. Nicola was in John's office, loading both the rifle and the shotgun. She whirled as the door from the kitchen opened and Sharon walked into the passage.

"Get back, get back," Noel shouted in despair, but Nicola came to the doorway and said smoothly, "Not at all, Sharon. Come right on in."

Sharon hesitated for only a second and then walked slowly up the passage. "In here." Nicola stepped outside the room and gestured with the rifle. "You too, Noel. You must have the constitution of an ox. I'd have sworn you wouldn't have been able to move by now."

"I can't—I can't." Noel made an effort to rise and fell heavily at Nicola's feet.

"Help her," Nicola said sharply, and she felt Sharon tugging at her arms, pulling her inside the office.

Nicola slammed the door shut with her foot. "All right then. Open the safe, Sharon. I want my money and my jewels. Do as I say."

"What's the matter with Noel?"

"She took an overdose. Don't worry about her. She killed John, didn't she?"

"No, she didn't. He's very much alive. She took me to the hospital and I saw him."

"You—did *what?* I told them to let no one in. I purposely—" She broke off and stared viciously at Noel who was leaning heavily up against the wall. "You couldn't let well alone. Well, now you're going to pay for it. And Sharon too. I'll use her as a hostage. I'll get away from here. Open that safe."

"I don't know how it works," Sharon said steadily.

"I'll tell you the combination. Pull the picture back."

Sharon hesitated and then stepped forward, following Nicola's instructions obediently. The safe was another innovation since Noel's time, built into the wall. Sharon pulled it open and Nicola said briskly, "I'll need some clothes, too. Go and pack a small suitcase for me. And don't think you can get away. If you're not back in five minutes I'll put a bullet in Noel."

"Run while you have the chance," Noel said draggingly. "A bullet won't make any difference to me and she'll kill you too once she doesn't need you any longer."

"On second thoughts, maybe I am putting too much faith in human nature," Nicola said crisply. "Empty that paper basket. I'll do without the case."

Sharon upended the basket. There were only one or two scraps of paper in it. She straightened. It was almost possible to read her intentions. Noel tensed as she suddenly hurled the basket right at Nicola's face but Nicola saw it coming and stepped aside, picking it up as it bounced harmlessly off the wall.

"A very rash thing to do, Sharon," she said coldly. "My finger might very well have tightened on this trigger." She emptied the contents of the safe into the basket. "Now we'll go—the back way."

"What about Noel?"

"She might live," Nicola said carelessly. "If they get her to the hospital in time."

Noel clenched her fists so hard it felt as if the glass was going through to the back of her hand.

Nicola wouldn't leave her without a parting shot. There was too much venom in her for that. She moaned, crashing forward to the floor, her outstretched hands breaking her fall to a certain extent but not enough to save her nose. For a moment the pain of that almost brought complete unconsciousness.

Nicola pulled her head up by the hair and examined her face, letting it fall again to give it a second knock. Noel felt the blood start to pour from her nose but as Nicola turned to herd Sharon out of the room she reached out and grabbed Nicola by the ankle, jerking it back.

Nicola cried out, stumbling a little but not completely losing her balance. Noel tried desperately to pull hard, crying out as Nicola jerked the rifle down hard on her hands and broke her hold.

She hadn't achieved anything, but Sharon had. She had snatched up the shotgun and was holding it steadily on Nicola.

"Now we'll go out—the front way, though."

"It takes nerve to kill," Nicola said softly and she brought the rifle up. "You wouldn't be able to do it in a thousand years. You proved it this afternoon. Now put that down. I think I've proved that I have the nerve."

"I'll do it if I have to," Sharon said stolidly.

Nicola laughed. She didn't believe her.

But Noel did. She scrabbled frantically on the carpet to gain purchase to pull herself out of range but Nicola put her foot on her back and squashed her puny efforts. "I won't kill you,

Sharon. I'll kill Noel—she'll be no good as a hostage and I'll need you."

The flesh on Noel's back cringed, her spine dissolving in pure undiluted fear. She could imagine Nicola's finger tautening on the trigger.

"Beg for your life, Noel. Tell Sharon I'm not bluffing."

Nicola hauled her up by the hair again and then pushed her viciously so that she fell sideways. "On your knees! Beg! I'll count to three, Sharon."

Noel stared straight into the cold black hole of the rifle. She couldn't look at Sharon.

When the blast came it lifted Nicola clean off her feet and hurled her back against the wall. Her body left a bloody stain right down the cream paper as she slid slowly downwards, her eyes wide and staring.

Sharon hadn't waited for her to start counting.

Noel swayed. She couldn't even stay on her knees. She dragged her gaze away from Nicola.

Sharon was standing like a statue, as white as alabaster.

"It's all right," Noel said foolishly as the door

was flung open and Powell rushed in. "It's perfectly all right." And she crashed forward once more, but this time there was no fake about it.

10

SHE knew she was in hospital before she opened her eyes. She felt desperately ill and there didn't seem to be any part of her body that didn't ache or hurt in one way or another.

She heard Dr. Shepherd's voice, brusque and testy. It faded and then bounced off her ears. "That's it. That's better. You open those eyes, Noel. I know you can hear me . . . There, you see."

She wasn't sure she did. It was an effort to bring him into focus. "You've not died on me yet, girl," he suddenly roared at her. "And you're not going to start now."

She tried to smile and didn't make it. His face receded, his voice dimming. She said weakly, "I'm not kicking so very well, am I, doctor? But don't worry . . . tomorrow's not here yet."

"You're damn right it's not. Come on now. Fight, girl. Don't give up at this stage."

This stage . . . and the next . . . and the

next. When they let her sleep at last she thought she would never wake up again but she opened her eyes to the chirping of a bird over the window and saw the sun slanting in through the half-drawn blinds.

A nurse was sitting in a chair at the side of the bed. She rose to her feet as Noel turned her head and within seconds Dr. Shepherd was bouncing in the room again.

"I guess it's tomorrow," Noel said.

"Tomorrow and tomorrow. It's Tuesday afternoon, my girl and you've nearly sent me to an early grave. How do you feel?"

"Peculiar."

"And is that so surprising? Sugar pills! I might have known. I did know, damn it. But that police inspector thought there was a chance it might work."

"So it would have done if Marion hadn't warned her," Noel said bitterly.

"You didn't tell me you'd gone to see them. If I'd known that—" He shrugged. "Oh, well. It's water under the bridge now. You'll have a scar on that hand of yours that will remind you of your folly for the rest of your life. And wait until you see Jonas. He very nearly annihilated me—and as for Powell . . . He's lucky he still has his job."

"You're trying to frighten me."

"Is that possible?" he asked gloomily. "Poor Jonas. He doesn't realise what lies ahead. Do you feel up to seeing him now?"

"I'm not afraid of him."

Dr. Shepherd snorted and went to the door.

"Sharon! What will happen to her?" Noel asked.

He pursed his lips. "Sharon! Well, I expect she'll manage to marry John. A resourceful young lady. She behaved with great presence of mind."

"They won't bring any kind of charge against her, will they? She saved my life."

"Yes, I think we can say that but, Noel . . . Nicola killed herself when the police burst in and she knew she couldn't get away."

"She—she did?" Noel faltered, remembering that look on Sharon's face as she watched Nicola slide down the wall with the life blasted out of her.

"She did," Dr. Shepherd said very firmly. "The case is now closed." He made his exit and Noel waited for Jonas.

She wasn't nervous. It was ridiculous to be

nervous. Of course Jonas would be annoyed with her. Annoyed? Too mild a word. Furious? One look at his face as he walked in and even that was a weak description.

"Don't look like that, Jonas," she said breathlessly. "I'm sorry I didn't tell you what I was going to do. I'm sorry I nearly got killed, I'm sorry for everything and I promise never to do any of it again. Never again. Never! Never!" She trailed off. His facial muscles hadn't relaxed by a centimetre. "You *do* still love me?" she asked forlornly.

"I feel like breaking every bone in your body," he said grimly.

"You still love me then," she said decidedly, and he groaned.

"Oh, Noel. How could you take such a risk?"

"I couldn't do it again," she assured him.

"I'll make sure you won't," he told her decidedly.

"That's enough," Dr. Shepherd said, entering briskly. "Five minutes I said."

"Five minutes!" Noel wailed in protest.

"Five minutes." Jonas kissed her lightly on her forehead. "We've all the time in the world ahead of us! There's no rush."

"No rush at all," Dr. Shepherd confirmed.

"You do as I tell you and you'll soon be out of here."

"This time," Noel said earnestly, "I will do *exactly* as you tell me."

Dr. Shepherd raised his eyebrows. "I can't believe my own ears. Is that Noel Clare speaking?"

"It certainly is." She smiled at Jonas. "I have a date to keep and I want to be in good shape for it."

"I'll be waiting for you—good shape or not." Jonas lifted his hand as Dr. Shepherd pointedly showed him to the door.

Noel closed her eyes and moved carefully into a more comfortable position. He'd be there. Yes, he'd be there. The waiting time was almost over.

THE END

A GENTEEL LITTLE MURDER
by Philip Daniels

Gilbert had a long-cherished plan to murder his wife. When the polished Edward entered the scene Gilbert's attitude was suddenly changed.

DEATH AT THE WEDDING
by Madelaine Duke

Dr. Norah North's search for a killer takes her from a wedding to a private hospital. She deals with the nastiest kind of criminal—the blackmailer and rapist!

MURDER FIRST CLASS
by Ron Ellis

A new type of criminal announces his intention of personally restoring the death penalty in England. Will Detective Chief Inspector Glass find the Post Office robbers before the Executioner gets to them?

THE MONTMARTRE MURDERS
by Richard Grayson

Inspector Gautier of Sûreté investigates the disappearance of artist Théo, the heir to a fortune. Then a shady art dealer is murdered and the plot begins to focus on three paintings by a seemingly obscure artist.

GRIZZLY TRAIL
by Gwen Moffat

Miss Pink, alone in the Rockies, helps in a search for missing hikers, solves two cruel murders and has the most terrifying experience of her life when she meets a grizzly bear!

BLINDMAN'S BLUFF
by Margaret Carr

Kate Deverill had considered suicide. It was one way out—and preferable to being murdered. Better than waiting for the blow to strike, waiting and wondering . . .

BEGOTTEN MURDER
by Martin Carroll
When Susan Phillips joined her aunt on a voyage of 12,000 miles from her home in Melbourne, she little knew their arrival would germinate the seeds of murder planted long ago.

WHO'S THE TARGET?
by Margaret Carr
Three people whom Abby could identify as her parents' murderers wanted her dead, but she decided that maybe Jason could have been the target. Then Abby was attacked in the old ruins and she wondered if she could be wrong after all.

THE LOOSE SCREW
by Gerald Hammond
After a motor smash, Beau Pepys and his cousin Jacqueline, her fiancé and dotty mother, suspect that someone had pre-arranged the death of their friend. But who, and why, and above all, how?

SANCTUARY ISLE
by Bill Knox
Chief Detective Inspector Colin Thane and Detective Inspector Phil Moss are sent to a bird sanctuary off the coast of Argyll to investigate the murder of the warden.

THE SNOW ON THE BEN
by Ian Stuart
Although on holiday in the Highlands, Chief Inspector Hamish MacLeod begins an investigation when a pistol shot shatters the quiet of his solitary morning walk. And then one of his suspects is found drowned.

HARD CONTRACT
by Basil Copper
Private detective Mike Farraday is hired by Eli Dancer to obtain settlement of a debt from Minsky. But Minsky is killed before Mike can get to him. A spate of murders follows.